chinese **ransom**

chinese **ransom**

denis **miller**

AESOP Modern Fiction
Oxford

AESOP Modern Fiction
An imprint of AESOP Publications
28 Abberbury Road, Oxford OX4 4ES, UK
www.aesopbooks.com

A catalogue record of this book is
available from the British Library.

ISBN: 978-1-910301-40-1

Preamble

Mexico

A S KEN LAWSON, the narrator in these pages, and until recently, a long-time government servant,[*] I have set down in Chapters 6 to 27 (the last) the corpus of the story touching on my own involvement. The first few chapters are the result of individual after-the-event talks with the handful of main characters involved in the story. This account is a sequel to *'The Chinese Jade Affair'* (published by Milton House/Mondadori 1975) written under my pen name of 'Denis Miller'.

Although the present tale is similarly set in the 1970s (and most is written in first-person narrative straight from memory backed by my notes at the time), the events, action, political double-dealing are all still relevant today. Certain brand and place names may in the best, literal sense 'date' the book; for example, there is the mention of 'Peking', but in the '70s if 'Beijing' cropped up in normal conversation, you would either be speaking Chinese or you would be in very specialist company.

So, my hope as the hard-working narrator, is that if the story is unashamedly 'retro', it is authentically so – and is written to entertain those readers who may like to travel with Ken Lawson in his momentous assignment.

*

---

[*] Employed by WRU (World Research Unit), an off-shoot of MI6, which HMG declines to acknowledge.

5

I am not very good at embroidery but, taking my time, the upper of the canvas slipper on which I have been sewing is coming along nicely – and, as a priority, I have been writing *Chinese Ransom*.

Of course, the atmosphere is conducive to such relaxing pastimes – the still, balmy air of Cuernavaca, the quiet mood of the modest hacienda itself, with the patio shaded by an orange-flowered Indian Laurel tree, and then the low balustrade covered by white Cadena de Amor. A few steps lead down to the greenest lawn imaginable which, forty yards away, is bordered by a stone wall – old but in good repair, and adorned by sprays of purple Bougainvillea. On the left, sunk into a stretch of lawn, is a well-stocked ornamental fish-pond and (separate) small swimming pool. The latter adjoins the patio, but is discreetly screened by Oleander and Poinsettia bushes. Everything is in flower, because it is always springtime in Cuernavaca.

Chapter 1

THROUGH THE FINE wire meshing of the side window frames came the unmistakeable change in the tempo of the after-dinner conversation. The young gardener noticed it at once. He didn't understand what was being said then or before, but he recognised the signal and, as usual, it sounded a little after midnight. The meshing kept the mosquitoes at bay, reduced the air-flow by forty per cent but scarcely affected the happy burble of a dozen people well wined and dined.

He stood up quickly with a muttered comment to his companion sitting against the trunk of an old Magnolia tree on the edge of the lawn at the rear of the house. A slim figure wrapped in a sari, with a comb working through shining waist-length hair, gracefully slipped away to the garden side gate.

The Thai boy walked towards the front door of the house, turned on a hose and set about watering the lush display of flowers and shrubs in the forecourt. There was nothing here that really needed attention after the usual seasonal downpour at four o'clock that afternoon, but he was sure to be seen doing something 'useful' when the main door opened, and Mr. Dobell, or his wife, would usher out the guests. This happened at least once a week. The gardener was well aware that his 'system' fooled nobody, but having started it six months ago, he now felt embarrassed to stop it.

He liked Henry Dobell who he considered to have learned a lot about Thailand since his arrival a year ago.

The young Thai didn't know of course that, with diplomatic 'cover' as a First Secretary, Dobell was in fact the MI6 Head of Station in Bangkok; in any case, even if *had* known, it would not have affected the Thai's hopes of being asked to take on some chauffeuring of the air-conditioned Rover 3500; driving such an elegant car appealed to him more than gardening.

However, he didn't like 'Madame' who anyway had her own smaller car; one of the reasons was that, through the grapevine of local staff who work for *farang** households, he knew that Marthe Dobell had rendezvous several times a month with gentlemen in apartments on the other side of town.

The front door opened. Dobell was there, a rather slight but athletic form. To the Thai boy, he seemed to have a gentle manner but with an unspoken authority recalling that of a senior Buddhist monk. Without waiting to be asked, the boy turned off the water and then ran to open the driveway gates.

While the guests lingered and milled around the forecourt, reluctant to embus, Henry Dobell remained in the doorway. He was in his early fifties, but looked younger. He was tired and rather fed up – as usual after such parties; he knew it would be another ten minutes before all the visitors had left. There was much polyglot fare-welling going on, and amidst the babble Dobell heard '*Spokoynoy nochi!*' – badly pronounced. He winced. In fact, he was well qualified to judge; he spoke excellent Russian and was an expert on Soviet affairs. He had several times acted as advisor/interpreter during the visits of various British Ministers to Moscow.

---

* Any foreigner in Thailand is known as a *farang*.

Marthe was there doing her duty, but drawn-out departure scenes exasperated both her and Dobell. The latter suddenly called out in a surprisingly strong bass voice 'Goodnight all – and look after your wives!' As a ragged chorus of approval answered, he waved briefly and turned back into the house. If he had been a little abrupt, Dobell thought that he would be forgiven, as there was one more guest who had remained inside.

He found him standing under one of the two large ceiling fans softly thudding round. The man was mopping his face with a coloured silk handkerchief. It had been a shirt-sleeve dinner, but Charles Houghton was a visitor from London who had arrived only that day. It takes a week or more to adjust to the humid heat of Bangkok.

'That's not the best place to stand, Charles ...'

'I know,' replied Houghton, gazing up at the propeller revolving in a slightly eccentric way, 'If that thing fell, it would cut you in half!'

Henry Dobell smiled. 'Oh, it's not that. I understand it's been in that state for fifteen years, ever since one of our drunken colleagues used to play fan cricket ... and he had the idea to use full beer cans instead of empty ones.'

Houghton chuckled, trying to think who the rash spirit might have been.

'No,' said Dobell, 'the best ventilated part of the room is over there ...' He pointed to a corner.

They moved across and sat down in worn rattan-ware easy chairs which squeaked in protest, but were very comfortable; the one Houghton used protested more because he was a heavily built man, and middle-age had added to his weight.

An elderly Thai woman, padding after them on gnarled bare feet, put an ice-bucket containing Heinekens bottles on a handy low table. She smiled 'Goodnight', and Dobell had a kind word for her.

'You're quite right,' said Houghton as his host poured the beer, 'There's a marvellous current of air here.'

'It's something to do with aeronautics and the result of a lot of careful research on my part, moving the furniture around—'

Houghton, looking over Dobell's shoulder, suddenly stood up. Marthe Dobell came towards them. She was a tall, handsome woman more than ten years younger than her husband.

'I've just come to say goodbye, Charles ... It was nice to see you again. Can't you really stay longer than one night?'

'No, I have to be in Kuala Lumpur tomorrow.' He thought Marthe was very desirable indeed – even without the added attraction of a slight accent which betrayed her German origins. 'But I'll be back soon no doubt. Thanks so much for a splendid evening, Marthe!'

She smiled and turned away. 'I'll leave you to it.' She had not said goodnight to her husband.

'I won't keep him long, Marthe.'

'Oh, don't worry – there's more beer outside ...'

It could have been a casual, understanding remark, but somehow the tone was wrong, and Houghton had the feeling that Marthe had only just failed to say something more obviously off-hand. She left, and the men sat down again.

After an uncertain pause, Dobell pushed a box of cigars towards Houghton. It would be his second Havana of the evening, but the duty-free aspect won the day and he lit up with relish. While attending to this, a mechanical humming noise came down the stairs; then the bedroom door closed.

'I note that at least you sleep in air-conditioned comfort!' It was an innocent quip from Houghton, but almost as it slipped out, he wished he had kept quiet. Rumour had it that all was not well in the Dobell household. For Henry, it had been a second marriage enthusiastically welcomed and blessed by friends and colleagues. The first had been brief and had ended almost twenty years earlier. And until Marthe's arrival on the scene three years ago, it seemed that Dobell was set on a bachelor's life.

'Not exactly ...' Dobell smiled easily. 'That's Marthe's room – I sleep with a fan.'

'Rough deal, old man, if it's anything like that one,' Houghton said, looking at the ceiling. The weak joke eased over an awkward moment. After some chuckles, he added: 'Can we talk here?'

'Yes, of course. The Thais I employ don't understand enough, and I doubt that the enemy is crawling around in the bushes outside. The gardener has a girlfriend who flits in and out at odd times – it's charming—'

'Henry, I'm afraid it's going to be a bit of a disappointment to you.'

'Oh?'

'But there is a brighter side,' Houghton added quickly.

'What's the disappointment?'

Even in the coolest part of the room, Houghton was still sweating freely. He swigged a mouthful of beer, dabbed at his face with the now very damp handkerchief, and then wiped his bushy moustache with two decisive strokes on either side.

'London won't have him as a defector.'

Dobell stared at his visiting colleague. It was unbelievable – as if a Fourth Division football club had turned down the free offer of a recycled George Best. Dobell sipped at the Heinekens while his mind did somersaults. He was used to dealing with surprises in his working day; by some odd reflex, he tended not to show any outward reaction. It was just the way he was made.

'Why not?' he asked gently.

'In the present climate, the Foreign Office will not jeopardise our relations with Peking. As you know, there are some major commercial projects in the pipeline ...'

'Charles, how long is it since we've had a Chinese defector – and especially somebody as important as the Number Two of a diplomatic mission?'

'I know, I know – at Head Office we're all behind you. But it's a political thing – the Foreign Office ... And the decision is the Minister's, so it's final.'

Dobell stood up and walked away to attend to a mundane need. 'Help yourself to more beer,' he called over his shoulder. Back in the room, he saw that Houghton had given him a refill, too.

'Thanks ... Cheers!' Dobell put his glass down. 'And what is the "bright side"?'

'It's agreed that he should be run as an agent.'

There was silence while Dobell mulled over the news. An over-ambitious wall-lizard fell with a soft plop twelve feet to the parquet nearby. Houghton looked at it with some distaste. The lizard seemed none the worse for the adventure and after taking stock of the new perspective, slithered across the polished floor as if swimming furiously against the current. Then it advanced up the more adhesive wall in swift, darting runs.

Outside there was a faint sizzling noise of insects and the persistent flutter of blind, incredulous moths against the window netting. The Thai gardener, now alone, was half dozing under the Magnolia tree. It was all very tropical, and Houghton waited, sweating profusely.

'What you really mean,' said Dobell quietly, 'is that we use the promise of a safe-haven – which in truth doesn't exist – to lever this man into spying for us in his present post.'

'Correct.'

'And the Foreign Office would accept that?'

'They don't want to know about it – they just don't want a defector!'

'Do you like trumpets?' Dobell said suddenly. Houghton, more than a little surprised, nodded his head politely as any guest would. Dobell got up and fiddled with an expensive Telefunken apparatus built into a cabinet. Another second or two, giving the visitor time to dispense the rest of the beer, and the sound of Handel's trumpets – great banks of them – seemed to come from every corner of the room. Houghton looked alarmed.

'It's square, exhilarating music,' Dobell said.

'It's very *loud* music,' replied Houghton, 'You'll wake Marthe!'

'She won't hear it – not with the air-conditioning ...' Dobell said with the trace of a smile. But he did turn the volume down and went back to his seat.

'We run the risk of losing him altogether, you know.'

'Yes – everybody realises that.' Houghton sounded vexed.

'Another point,' Dobell continued, 'As you know, I've dealt with several defectors in the past. More or less straightforward. They were of course people who wanted to come over. We helped them, and it has always been one of the better aspects of the government's attitude to accept such cases, regardless of the political situation. But the idea of dangling a non-existent "Welcome to the UK" promise to get this Chinese to work for us strikes me as indecent even for ... for ...'

'Even for SIS?'[*] prompted Houghton. 'Yes, but you—'

'I haven't finished,' broke in Dobell, 'I might be phrasing my objections more strongly if it were not that the man is due to be posted to Europe any day now – and happily I'll be far away from all this ... this nastiness!'

Houghton looked very uncomfortable. He leaned forward and thrust his hand into the bucket of half-melted ice and strained the water into his glass.

'Good heavens, man – I'll get some more beer!' Dobell stood up to see about it.

'No, no more beer thanks. Water will do nicely. I suppose this *is* drinkable?' Houghton said as his glass filled.

'If you can live with your hand, the water is all right, delivered in hygienic casks twice a week. Fifteen million Thais thrive on water from the mains, but we, for some reason, have to drink purified stuff in bottles.'

Houghton laughed, and still with a smile on his face, he said: 'The other news is that we want you to come back to look after him.'

Again there was no visible reaction from Dobell.

'Why don't you put a specialist onto this?' he said after a second's pause, 'I haven't got the right feel where

---

[*] Secret Intelligence Service. 'SIS' is often used between colleagues and familiarly for 'MI6'.

a Chinese is concerned. It would be different with Soviets and East Europeans – I know a bit about them. But a Chinese ...? And this would be a very high-grade affair.'

'It's gone very well so far -'

'Balls! Let's be honest, I've done almost nothing – the man has practically thrown himself at me!'

Houghton coughed lightly. 'Admittedly, there's nobody available at the moment.'

'Ah ... Then why don't you go off-section – WRU, for example. They're an unpredictable lot, but they have some good people—'

'Since the last fiasco, there's nobody there either!'

Dobell looked at the other man in surprise; then he suddenly remembered that after a recent scandal involving another Chinese and WRU, Houghton had no love of this shady subsidiary of MI6. That affair had ended in a Whitehall uproar and Charles Houghton, because of his particular responsibilities at Head Office, had taken it very badly. Dobell knew that Houghton, a man of certain rigid principles, had taken a violent dislike to the WRU operative concerned, one Ken Lawson.

'So, if I've got it right,' Dobell said blandly, sliding over a prickly subject, 'for overriding political reasons, HMG is not prepared to receive a high-level Chinese defector full of fascinating tales to be milked at leisure, but, at the risk of losing all, the plan is to convert this disenchanted Maoist into a secret agent?'

'That's it,' said Houghton briskly, and stretched himself in the rattan chair, which crackled and creaked as some 14 stones' weight was redistributed.

'I think it's fantasy,' said Dobell, 'like the promise of asylum that is very unlikely to be granted.'

Houghton stood up and yawned. 'I take it you agree,'

he said. He wanted to have it cut and dried for his cable to London in the morning.

'Oh, you can count on me to do my little bit,' Dobell said and went to turn off the record-player. 'But I must say it's a bloody funny way to run a Secret Service.'

When the music stopped, the half-asleep Thai boy looked at his watch. 1.30 am. He waited another few minutes, watching the house. A bit disappointed when the downstairs lights were switched off, he was hoping that Dobell would be taking the car to drive the last guest back to a hotel, and he would be there, the miraculous night-watchman, to open the gates.

But the moustachioed *farang* was evidently staying the night. The young Thai walked slowly back to his quarters and wondered if he was not taking his hoped-for chauffeuring prospects too seriously.

Chapter 2

THE CATHAY HOUSE is one of Bangkok's second-rank hotels. It is a square, office-block building of functional appearance, which sits a little back from a busy thoroughfare. Not in the same class as the airline connected palaces grouped in the commercial centre – inasmuch as the amorphous city has a centre at all – it is nevertheless busy with a fast turnover of an international clientèle.

Located in a nondescript part of town, it is fifteen minutes closer to the airport than most other large hotels and convenient for those visitors having business with Thai government ministries, many of which are spread around the nearby area graced by temples with names like 'Wat Po' and 'Wat Preakaew'.

The Cathay House caters for tourists – Asian and European – who are not in the luxury class, businessmen who are making a bit on travel expenses and groups of working-level foreign officials who pour into the country to attend conferences – particularly in the context of United Nations projects involving Thailand.

In short, it's neither a sensation in modern living nor has it the scruffy folklore of the smaller, cheaper places that proliferate downtown in what is virtually the 'Chinese' area. It suited Henry Dobell's purpose very well.

It was one of several similar hotels where Dobell, using a different name, took a room once every ten days or so. This was the system by which he could meet, anonymously and in some security, two or three of his lesser informants who were part of Dobell's bread-and-butter earnings. He had other arrangements for dealing with more important contacts. Before his posting to Thailand, he had operated for the best part of twenty years in the restrictive conditions of Eastern Europe, so he knew what he was doing.

A few days after Charles Houghton left Bangkok, Dobell had a routine meeting at the Cathay House. He spent the afternoon talking to a local businessman, half Thai, half Lao, who ran a transport concern plying between Bangkok and Vientiane. The business did quite well and even when it flagged, the ideally placed transporter engaged in a little – but very profitable – gold smuggling.

Dobell's interest in this man stemmed from the latter's mobility in Laos – he often trekked out of Vientiane into the country – and from the fact that he was distantly related to one of the princely families in charge of Laos. In sum, he knew a lot about Lao affairs. Dobell was not unduly impressed by his personal credentials, because many Laotians one meets seem to be distantly related to one of the princely families. Nevertheless this always happy traveller often had something useful to report. And oven if there was no real political content, whatever the transporter had to say was invariably entertaining.

After being 'entertained' for a couple of hours during the afternoon, Dobell had no further official need for the hotel room that week and he could pack his overnight bag and leave. But he didn't check out of the Cathay House after the business was finished. And he had rarely done so, either at this place or other hotels, for about the last six months. He had booked the room for an extra day – and neither this nor similar extensions figured in any accounting.

Dobell called at his office for an hour and returned again to the hotel in the early evening. As always for any of these non-official excursions, he changed his normal appearance in a superficial but effective way. It was in no sense a great theatrical disguise, but merely a precaution to reduce the chances of being recognised by a passing acquaintance, Australian cousins on an Asian walkabout or his gardener – given the fact that he was known in this or that hotel under another name.

The Hawaiian shirt, soft, light-coloured Trilby seen on golf courses and the large, very dark glasses were just not Henry Dobell's style; he would have to be standing next to an unnaturally perceptive friend in the lift to be recognised. Dobell didn't use the lift, in any case. He walked up the stairs to the third-floor room.

He showered and put on a light silk bathrobe in the fashion of a Japanese *happi* coat; this could also have been part of the charade, but it would certainly have raised the eyebrows of the daily help back home at West Byfleet, Surrey, England.

After pouring himself a whisky – a long drink topped up with three-quarters of a tumbler of water – Dobell loaded a portable player with one of the several records he had brought along in his briefcase. It was scarcely hi-fi equipment, but it made enough of Ravel for him to enjoy.

He sat down and lit the fourth of the five cigarettes that he now allowed himself each day. Previously he had been a two – sometimes three – packet man and it was an odd facet of his character that having made the awful decision some years ago about cigarettes in general, instead of giving up altogether he settled for the more difficult regime of gradual reduction. He had now reached what he believed to be the ideal consumption. Five a day was a reassuring habit, the health risk was reduced and every draw was savoured fully. In fact he was hovering uncertainly on the edges of the cigar smoker's kingdom – the real thing, not the debased transatlantic version of chomping and chewing on the things all day long, but one or two after sundown, carefully chosen and each one au event rather than a mindless craving. Henry Dobell had always tried to organise and discipline his pleasures.

At 8.30 p.m. Dobell got up quickly to answer a knock on the door. A good-looking young man in his early twenties stood there smiling, almost shyly, at Dobell.

'I bring the new Arrau, Henry…'

Dobell smiled too. 'Good,' he said softly and took the young Thai's arm to usher him into the room. As he closed the door he added. 'You should say "*I have brought*" – not "*bring*" although I can't tell you why.'

*

It was just before midnight when the Thai student left. The room was already darkened and Dobell pulled the curtain a little to one side to watch his friend walk across the parking area below to collect his motor-scooter always left in the same spot; the boy was slim and lithe and Dobell thought that the strange modern word 'unisex' has a special meaning in Thailand. The Thai looked back up at the building once and then he was astride the scooter, heading for the exit.

There was quite a lot of traffic on the adjoining main road but little movement in the well-lit forecourt of the hotel. As the Thai turned out of the exit-way, Dobell noticed another man of much bigger build – a European – who was half walking, half running towards a motorcycle parked some twenty yards from the exit. He had actually kicked the engine into life, when from the other side of the parking area a car's headlights flashed several times. The motorcyclist hesitated then dismounted. Dobell was suddenly very alert indeed.

The man walked towards the car from which another European emerged and the two stood in consultation under a neon lamp – which might have been made for the purpose. Dobell didn't know the impetuous wild one who had been about to take off into the Bangkok night in pursuit of a Thai student, but he did recognise the other man who had got out of the car.

Dobell, transfixed by the window, concluded that the motorcyclist had misunderstood his instructions and was now being put in his place by…

Alexander Karpov, listed variously in Soviet embassies around the world as 'Attaché', 'Special Assistant', 'Commercial Advisor', and sometimes he wasn't listed at all, as in the Bangkok Embassy of the USSR. He was a person comrade Counsellors, and in some cases even Ambassadors, tipped their hats to when nobody was looking. In short, he was not somebody to tangle with in a dark alley. Or even in the brightly lit forecourt of the Cathay House Hotel in Bangkok.

Dobell stood rigidly still for some seconds; then he let the curtain fall back into place.

He turned slowly and refilled his glass for the first time since the early evening. He put another record on the machine and sat down, reflective, in high gear, and appalled at what he had seen.

The Thai student himself was not of the slightest

Intelligence use to the Russians – or anybody else. The dreadful awareness of what this really meant gnawed at Dobell's innards; he knew that the only conceivable reason for the Karpov team's interest in the boy was his association with him, Dobell...

If they were alert to the Thai boy, they were also well aware of his own presence in the hotel. And that could only mean one thing.

He knew it couldn't be a 'probe' microphone mounted in a wall or the ceiling from an adjoining room, because they wouldn't have had time to install it; nor could it be the telephone, which is easy enough to make 'live' because, of course, the monitoring post would be the hotel exchange to which it was most unlikely that the Russians had access.

Dobell guessed that it would be a transmitting microphone, less than the size of a matchbox, rapidly put in place and easily hidden.

He set about a methodical search of the room, high and low, in the folds of curtains, corners of furniture and he even had the mattress off the bed. Recesses of cupboards and lockers revealed nothing but dust and dead insects and one cheap tiepin, long lost and forgotten.

It was almost 2 a.m. After an hour of fruitless effort Dobell felt hot, dirty and tired; his mood for the moment was as much irritation as apprehension. He *knew* it must be there somewhere. They would never pass up such chance; he had to find it to satisfy himself – although half hoping that finally he hadn't found it, because there wasn't anything to find.

He subsided on the bed, and lit the last of his five cigarettes and looked vaguely round the room. An absurd irrelevancy struck him: how many years was it since he had seen one of those stern notices saying: 'Guests are asked to refrain from smoking in bed'? In this room, for example, there were glass ashtrays conveniently placed on the bedside lockers as well as a few more on the desk and dressing-table unit. In fact the place was equipped for a chain-smoking family. There was an even bigger receptacle on the desk – a real spittoon affair made of some opaque plastic and which seemed to be a highly popular brand; it was in vulgar taste, to Dobell's mind. He scowled and blew smoke at it.

Then he stared at the offending object as he realised that the reason he knew it was so 'popular' was that he had noticed the same item in several other hotels he had been frequenting recently.

He slid off the bed, a man inspired. At first he didn't touch it, but crouched down to examine it closely. A thin line round the base suggested that it was constructed in two parts to no normal purpose in an ashtray made of moulded plastic. Dobell studied the latticework design on two sides of the base – also superfluous décor – with an interest that was momentarily gleeful.

He turned the volume of the record-player up and carried the ashtray very close to the speaker; he saw through the latticework that the base was hollow. There was no real need to unscrew the base, but Dobell did so, still holding it very close to the speaker to drown the noise of his tampering.

There it was, lurking in the cavity like some sinister bloated beetle, a small black pack of no doubt highly efficient Russian invention, which had been transmitting enough over the last few months to ensure that Dobell's distinguished career of 25 years would soon end in shame and ignominy. Unless, as he would certainly be pressured to do, Dobell became 'useful' to the Russians.

The listening post would be in the hotel – not necessarily in an adjacent room but somewhere within a radius of twenty yards. It didn't matter much to Dobell where it was. He screwed the ashtray together again, replaced it on the desk and then reduced Claudio Arrau's majestic rendering the Prokofiev concerto to a mere normal late-night listening level.

He lay back on the bed again and now that he was sure, as always happened in his moments of crisis, he felt engulfed by an awful calm; it was this that made some say Dobell 'had no heart' or was 'a cold fish'. Others who were closer to him knew this wasn't true; he did suffer, react and storm inwardly – his peculiarity was that it was rarely apparent.

And Dobell had indeed suffered – all his adult life. He had always been aware of course of a particular aspect of his make-up, but it had been effectively smothered and disciplined both by the circumstances of his work and also by his own conception of 'acceptable' conduct. In fact, working in a dedicated, high-pressure way for so long in the very restrictive atmosphere of East European capitals had helped him to ignore the issue. It was the vastly different climate of a permissive Asian city that had done for him.

Dobell had asked for the Bangkok posting – because it was a new area for him after Europe and one long spell in Cuba. When his tour in Thailand ended, he had hoped before retirement for a grace and favour posting in Madrid, Rome or Paris, where, at the top of the pile, his main chore would be to count his staff once a week and then go off to lunch with enthusiastic stalwarts of the *Direccion General de Seguridad, Servizio Informazione*

Difesa or the *Direction de la Surveillance du Territoire (DST)*, as the case may be.

Since 1 a.m. that morning the prospect had brutally changed. Dobell had taken a calculated risk and, rather against the odds, had lost. He had certainly been affected by the sudden release from operating in Communist territory for so long, and Thailand, relatively speaking, had seemed easy.

He had not been careless in regard to the official use of the hotels – the arrangement was considered averagely secure (especially in this city), but his private use of the rooms, he knew, was inexcusable, quite apart from the implications of the nature of this 'private' use.

Henry Dobell had never thought of himself as a loser, despite his ambiguous personal situation over the years. Indeed with an O.B.E. already to his name and probably a higher honour on retirement, nobody else thought of him as a loser either. As he lay on the bed sipping at the rest of the now tepid whisky-water, he accepted the fact with curious detachment that, this time, he *was* a loser. It was only a matter of time before the Russians cashed in.

Dobell's thoughts turned to his recent conversation with that pompous but rather deep man Charles Houghton, who had come bearing the astonishing news that Head Office in London didn't want a *bona fide* high-level Chinese defector, but they were prepared to use the '*bona fide*' element to try to turn the man into a spy. He recalled, too, that he was due to meet this Chinese in two days' time – but not, of course, in this or any other hotel. Dobell thought for another half an hour. As he had told Houghton, he would do his little bit.

This included, for a start, opening the door quietly and walking to the end of the corridor to a dial 'house phone'. Dobell called his own room number and then left the receiver dangling. He walked quietly back and picked up the telephone which was buzzing by the bed.

'Hello … it's three o'clock in the morning! What do you … I see … Well, if it's *that* important we can do it here. I suppose I can keep the room for another few weeks… No, not now but I'll check with the front desk first thing in the morning … Don't worry … Thanks for calling … Goodnight.'

Dobell couldn't really be sure, of course, that this piece of fiction would be picked up. But he assumed the Soviet recording apparatus somewhere in the hotel would be working round the clock. At least it would confuse the monitors and tie up some staff for the next fortnight.

It was an off-the-cuff, last-minute diversion from a newly qualified 'loser' who still hadn't forgotten how good he had been for the last 25 years.

Chapter 3

A WEEK LATER, in the early hours one morning, a Thai Police jeep pulled in to check a Rover 3500, which had pulled off a deserted stretch of road seven miles outside Bangkok. The car was parked untidily on the mud verge and although the motor was stopped, the headlights were still on and the driver's door was open.

The Patrol was casual in its first survey and sundry ribald interpretations of the scene were bandied about; the approach was also tentative because the Rover, after all, had diplomatic registration plates. However, with still no sign of the driver after ten minutes, growing puzzlement gave way to wide-eyed alertness and action as the Thai police discovered signs of a struggle: a scrap of suiting torn off on an inside door handle, a broken gold cufflink on the floor of the car together with a mess of other items – maps, papers, and a few tools – which seemed to have fallen from the open glove-box. Then they found a 9 mm Browning automatic jammed under the driver's seat.

The Thai police lieutenant in charge radioed Headquarters and within two minutes the Patrol learned that the owner of the Rover was a senior British diplomat. Shortly, other police vehicles arrived and a full-scale search of the area was underway.

Some thirty police fanned out in the semi-cultivated surrounds of tapioca plantations and patches of tropical scrub and trees. There was a lot of shouting and swinging of torches and hurricane lamps; this was partly to advise the diplomat that help was on the way and partly it was corporate encouragement to the faint-hearted squelching in the hot blackness through irrigation ditches and lush, dank vegetation. All the noise and thrashing about would intimidate the green kraits and cobras and anything else hiding there.

At daybreak two low-level helicopters were pounding their way back and forward across the terrain in support of the searchers below.

At midday the search was called off. Police experts, after examining the tyre imprints near the Rover, concluded that it had been forced off the road by another vehicle.

Henry Dobell was officially reported as having been abducted by persons unknown some time that night between 11.30 p.m. and 2.30 a.m.

.

Chapter 4

Paris

IN A VERY UPMARKET part of the city, the doorman at the Crazy Horse Cabaret at the bottom of *avenue George V* watched a very small car creeping along the pavement towards him. As it drew nearer, he saw that it had 'CD' plates. He gestured to a gap in the long line of parked vehicles, which would be just about enough to house an Austin Mini manoeuvred skilfully. He moved across to help direct the parking operation but this proved unnecessary as the Austin backed neatly into the space at the first try. He opened the door for the driver and was surprised to find that the latter was even taller than he was - and emerging from such a small run-about.

'*Le spectacle vient de commencer, monsieur...*'

The driver looked over his shoulder and grinned cheerfully at the doorman:

'*Moi, je vais à l'autre spectacle en face!*' he said with an affected American accent, and gesturing to a building across the street.

The other man laughed, but he was a little irritated to have let go a precious parking space to somebody who was not a customer after all. His main job was to ensure order and decorum among the crowd who queue to see the most beautiful girls in Europe peel it all off twice every night. It's all so slick and sophisticated that everybody can come away from the show with an easy conscience, claiming that it is all so slick and sophisticated.

Ian Potter locked the car and pushed his heavy-framed spectacles further up his nose and crossed the avenue in a few easy strides. In the hallway of the elegant early nineteenth-century building opposite the Crazy Horse, they gave him a ticket with the pencilled number 87 in return for his overcoat and he made his way up the wide staircase to the first-floor salon area, which is where the Embassy of the Chinese Peoples Republic in Paris holds its receptions.

Potter was late and the receiving line had already dispersed and would not re-form again for another half an hour when the hundred or so guests started to leave. Even the usual French butler figure in tails who announced the names of arrivals to a largely disinterested assembly had slipped away to a side pantry for a quiet smoke and a drink or two on the house.

The two interconnecting salons in use were crowded. Chinese Embassy receptions are always well attended – not only because for years now the Chinese have become the stars of the international scene and officials everywhere trip over one another in an unseemly rush to talk to Peking's emissaries, but also there is usually an abundant supply of excellent Chinese food at these gatherings.

Potter edged his way through the crowd towards a bar-buffet table at the rear, pausing here and there to greet acquaintances, including one or two Chinese whom he had met before casually on other social occasions.

He was there not because he had any special interest in Chinese affairs but rather in answer to a courtesy invitation brought about by his seniority in the British Embassy hierarchy as revealed by the Diplomatic List. In reality, under cover of being a senior British diplomat, Ian Potter was the head of the MI6 station in Paris. But there was no reason for the Chinese to know that, since he had never, as far as he knew, crossed their path professionally. He was basically an Arab man and his location in France will not unduly strain the reader's imagination.

So Potter was there at this Chinese Embassy reception as a matter of social duty; he had resolved to make the most of it by lapping up the Bollinger and feasting on the most succulent spring rolls in Paris.

By the buffet table, along which the knowledgeable were jammed tight, Potter sipped at his champagne appreciatively but was disappointed to see that although there were still giant heaps of steamed prawns and chicken noodles, the celebrated spring rolls had long since been snapped up by earlier arrivals.

Potter was still peering at the well-laden table when he felt a touch at his elbow. He looked round to find a smiling Chinese at his side, dressed in a dark-blue tunic uniform. He was a slim, tall man in his early forties.

'You are Mr Potter of the British Embassy, I think...'

Potter agreed, vaguely surprised, while shaking hands with the Chinese. 'My name is Tan,' the latter said. 'I am the new Counsellor here...' He handed a name-card to Potter. 'It is an old card – I have only been in Paris a few days...' Potter slipped the card into his breast pocket without examining it. His attention was drawn entirely to the man himself who was still talking. Chinese diplomats do not normally rush up to Western guests and make themselves known in this forward way. It is always the other way round.

'You have a drink, I see. What about some food?'

'As a matter of fact, I was hoping t find some spring rolls left...' said Potter.

At the mention of 'spring rolls' several English-speaking heads in the immediate vicinity snapped round, but they decided it was a false alarm. Counsellor Tan, however, leaned across the long buffet table and gave a brief order to one of the Chinese staff. Before Tan had finished refilling Potter's glass from a handy bottle of Bollinger, the Chinese in a neat white jacket returned from a hole in the wall with a fresh helping of everybody's favourite dish. These were not the packages of greasy cardboard stuffed with soggy leftovers that sometimes pass for spring rolls in Chinese restaurants in the West, but something of a mixture of crisp bean sprouts, finely diced pork and seasoning, wrapped in a light, almost fragile golden-brown, batter casing.

'Ah...' said Potter, and pushed his spectacles further up his nose again in a habitual gesture that accompanied the onset of decision-making or purposeful action. Counsellor Tan had taken a disposable cardboard plate from a stack on the table and, in a few deft chopstick movements, loaded it with the choicest morsels off the pile. He then proffered the plate to the enthusiastic Potter.

There was a sudden surge from behind towards the table and in the jostling Potter was obliged to raise his champagne glass above the throng. It was the nearest diplomats get to stampeding. He retreated a few steps to the centre of the room and the good-humoured Tan followed him with the provisions.

As Tan rather carefully handed him the throwaway plate, Potter became aware that he was being offered something in addition to the best spring rolls in the Western hemisphere. Underneath he could feel either a thick folded sheet of paper or an envelope. Tan had hung onto the plate just long enough to be sure that Potter had noticed.

Now Potter, very well adjusted though he was to the vagaries of the Arab temperament, was wholly ignorant of things Chinese and a gaffe at this point might be forgiven. But Potter was also an experienced Intelligence Officer. The natural reaction – temptation even – for an 'innocent' would be to fish out the oddly placed envelope, examine it in a carefree way in full view of the company with a remark such as: 'I say, what's this, Mr Tan – I think I've got some of your mail here...'

But Potter was no innocent. With proper thanks, he took the plate with its unusual under-hang, sipped again at his champagne and put the glass down on a window-ledge. Munching on one of those golden-brown goodies, he turned and looked steadily at the expectant Mr Tan. Then Potter made the obvious remark: 'Your spring rolls are awfully good, you know.'

Counsellor Tan smiled easily and with a courteous word of excuse turned to join a group of long-robed francophone Africans.

Ian Potter walked back into the crowd by the table and while advancing amongst this preoccupied and animated company, he detached the envelope and put it in his pocket. After another glass of champagne and a leisurely progression towards the exit, he left to collect his Austin Mini.

He switched on the overhead light and examined the envelope. It was blank and unsealed. On the single sheet inside was printed in biro a simple, explicit message: 'I WANT TO BE PUT IN CONTACT IMMEDIATELY WITH MR. K. LAWSON. WE WILL NOT DEAL WITH ANYBODY ELSE. IT CONCERNS MR. DOBELL.'

The message was unsigned, but it was perfectly clear that it was Counsellor Tan of the Chinese Peoples Government who was the author. The first thing that struck Potter (a minor irrelevance) was the use of the oddly formal 'Misters'. Then the full import of the note sank in.

'Good, God...' Potter murmured aloud. He sat quite still for some seconds staring unseeingly ahead. 'Good God,' he said again. A sudden rap on the driver's window made him start so much that he banged his bead on the roof – there was very little clearance.

The shock was compounded as Potter saw that it was the face of the Crazy Horse doorman peering into the glass. As Potter opened the window, unnerved and irritated, the other man was grinning.

'Nobody leaves our spectacle halfway through,' he said, 'so next time you—!

'Okay, okay,' said Potter shortly, 'I'm in a hurry!'

The doorman of the Crazy Horse watched the little Austin accelerate down the street. '*Salaud de diplomate*,' he said between his teeth.

By the time Potter was flinging the Mini round the well-lit death-trap known as Place de la Concorde on the way to his office, he decided, for a number of reasons, that he was not in so much of a hurry after all. He pulled in to a parking lot just opposite the Hotel Crillon to do some quiet reflection.

Potter examined the message again. It was bizarre in several respects. Although the affair had so far miraculously been kept out of the press, he knew of course that his colleague Henry Dobell had been abducted in Bangkok because there had been a worldwide All Posts Alert. But it was just the fact that a first lead should be discovered in Paris – Potter's nice, comfortable beat and so close to home – rather than in, say, Zanzibar.

The second surprise was to find the Chinese on the scene. Russians, East Europeans and even Arabs spend half their time exchanging secret massages, trailing around dark alleys and generally messing around with underhand methods. But the Chinese are rarely caught so engaged; perhaps they are so good that nobody gets to hear about it.

Another point was how had the Chinese known that he, Potter, was the appropriate recipient for such sensitive security information? It could only mean that they had correctly identified him as an MI6 officer. Potter was not unduly worried about this – everybody else knew, but it was just unreasonable that the Chinese should also know.

The aspect that really startled Potter was the specific demand that the ex-WRU man, Ken Lawson, be produced. He was well aware of Lawson's past and recent history, In fact Potter had watched from the sidelines during Lawson's last tangle with the Chinese, improbably involving a jade statuette – an affair that had earned the Special Operations Fund a great deal of money. Because of irregular conduct Lawson had officially been retired with no pension but unofficially he had been handsomely paid off – a decision fought tooth and nail by some and notably by Charles Houghton, the Director of China operations at Head Office.

Potter knew that Counsellor Tan's few words would provoke an uproar in London. It was almost 10 p.m. He decided not to send an immediate cable, which Houghton would have to go into the office to read and on which no effective action could be taken until the morning. Instead, he decided to go to London himself on the early morning flight, which would enable him to be at the office before the opening of business.

He wiped a patch clear on the steamed-up windscreen and drove quietly up the best known street in the world towards his apartment. Yes, it would no doubt be useful for him to be on hand in London when the bombshell was produced.

It was also true that Potter was two weeks overdue for a suit-fitting at Solomon and Burke in Jermyn Street.

'*Ça tombe bien,*' Potter said to himself, '*ça tombe bien...*'

Chapter 5

London

THERE ARE 32 different species of birds that inhabit
St James's Park. Charles Houghton over the years
had identified to his satisfaction 31. There
remained a small duck called the Lesser Teal, which had
so far escaped Houghton's keen eye.

It was midday and Houghton had just sat down on a
favourite bench that gave the widest views of the central
lake. Ten minutes earlier he had emerged from the inter-
ministerial Committee of Inquiry for Security Affairs
(CISA) in daily session to discuss the baffling
disappearance of a senior MI6 officer in Thailand.
Houghton arranged his bulky briefcase beside him and
hooked his umbrella on the back of the bench.

'Hello, Charles, I see that you like fresh air, too ...'
the rotund figure of Ralph Scott-Baker was approaching
on twinkling feet; a Foreign Office man, he had also been
at the CISA meeting and was the formal F.O. liaison with
MI6. For good reason he was known as 'The Supervisor'.

'I was just strolling back to the office when I spotted
you,' he said cheerfully. 'It's a nice day. Do you mind if I
sit with you for a moment?'

Houghton nodded a smile and moved his briefcase to
make room. The other man was waxing on about the joys
of London parks, and it was clear that he would be there
for some time yet. Houghton delved into his case and
pulled out a package.

'You can share my lunch, if you like – roast-beef
sandwiches?'

Scott-Baker looked at the proffered pile in some surprise. 'That's very decent of you. Are you sure you've got enough?' he said, and helped himself. Nice thin wholemeal bread and, inside, tender red meat with a dash of mustard – just what he liked.

'I do this quite often,' said Houghton half apologetically, '… a quick bite here and then I'm back at the office when everybody else is out, and the damned telephone stops ringing for a bit. It's the best hour of the day!'

'May I …? Scott-Baker was taking another sandwich. 'These CISA sessions are so vague; a week has gone by and there's still not the slightest trace of the man from any quarter.'

'I just don't understand it,' said Houghton glumly, 'as you heard this morning, the Thais are convinced he's been taken out of the country. They maintain that a European couldn't be kept in the area for so long without them hearing about it.'

'A live European, that is …' reflected Scott-Baker, while lifting the corner of his sandwich to check the contents. 'By the way, how's his wife taking it?'

'Oh, she's bearing up so far … Of course, I had her brought back.' Houghton looked sharply at the other man. 'She didn't really want to come, and I … er … well, she's staying with some friends of mine and—'

He broke off suddenly and stared across the lake. Scott-Baker looked slightly alarmed, but profited from the moment to take the last sandwich. Houghton suddenly rummaging in his brief-case; cursing softly, he pulled out a thermos flask, folders and a sheaf of papers before he found what he was looking for.

For a few seconds, he trained the binoculars on a

clump of vegetation in the middle of the lake and then dropped them away in an impatient gesture. 'It's another of those confounded Golden Eyes!' he snapped. He turned to find his companion staring at him in blank astonishment; the F.O. man had a half-eaten sandwich poised, immobile at his mouth.

'Ducks!' said Houghton briskly, by way of explanation, 'One of the little blighters here has been eluding me for years.'

Scott-Baker resumed his attack on the sandwich. 'I didn't know you were a birdwatcher, Charles…' he said and looked severely at the heap of highly classified papers strewn around his lunch seat. There were many others in addition to the 'limited' working brief for that morning's CISA meeting.

'Have been all m'life,' said Houghton with a smile. 'Like some coffee?' he added, holding the thermos in one hand and stuffing the papers back into the briefcase with the other.

'Thanks awfully – yes… I'm not running you short, am I?' Scott-Baker warmed his hands round the beaker and thought of something else.

'These wretched meetings start so early – they ruin the day. You can't get to the morning's cables before lunch…' The Supervisor paused and added a natural question: 'I suppose, Charles, that you go directly to the CISA from home every morning?'

'Yes, of course – it's much easier. Er… have you finished with the mug? … Thank you...' Houghton took his turn with the pre-sweetened Nescafé. 'What is so baffling,' he continued, 'is that the All Posts alert incidentally produced any number of British tax-dodgers in far-away places, a few unfortunates escaping from their wives and other Englishmen living in almost legal and exotic circumstances abroad, but not a hint about Dobell. To say nothing of the list of *mafiosi* we sift through every morning, which the American drag-net produces.'

Houghton packed up his briefcase. 'It doesn't make any sense,' he said. 'I'm rather inclined to think Dobell is dead – killed for some purely arbitrary or criminal motive.' He stood up and pointed his umbrella in a menacing way at the small, thickly planted island in the middle of the lake: 'I'll have that little ... that little ...'

'Duck?' prompted Scott-Baker.

'That little duck – one of these day...' Houghton smiled, waved away The Supervisor's thanks for the *al fresco* lunch and strode towards a building overlooking the Park.

*

'There's Ian Potter from Paris to see you, Mr Houghton. He's been waiting since ten this morning.' A middle-aged secretary looked expectantly at Houghton as he passed through her room to get to his own office. It was just after one o'clock.

'It's lunchtime, Flora – how many times must I tell you—'

'Mr Potter says it's very urgent...'

'Potter? ... Potter? He's from Paris, isn't he? What the devil does he want?'

'Shall I show him in, Mr Houghton?'

'Oh God... yes, all right.'

Potter in fact had been delayed at Orly because of fog and he had only just made it in time for what he knew to be the normal business opening time at Head Office. Already keyed-up, he had been fretting ever since to find that Houghton was absent at a meeting. The rules of the game are such that nobody was going to tell him that it was a CISA meeting about Dobell. So Potter drank a lot of coffee during the morning and telephoned his tailor twice. He felt frayed and less relaxed than he wanted to be as he delivered the news.

Houghton read the message calmly enough, put it on the desk and looked hard at his visitor. 'You were not drinking last night, I suppose?'

'Look,' said Potter. 'I have made a special effort at considerable personal inconvenience to come to London this morning instead of getting you out of bed late last night to read a priority cable. The fact that you were not here to receive me at ten o'clock is not my fault!'

This was strong talk in the face of Houghton, who was a powerful man in MI6; but Potter belonged to another Directorate and he knew that the importance of the news he brought gave him extra licence.

'Quite so, quite so...' said Houghton equably and studied the note again. 'Lawson...' he murmured, 'that's all I needed – Lawson…'

'There's also something about our missing colleague Henry Dobell, if I remember correctly,' said Potter mildly.

Suddenly Houghton's mood changed. He looked squarely at Potter and stroking his moustache said, 'Who is this Tan? You say he is new in Paris – where did he come from?'

Potter then knew, for the first time in many years, what it felt like not to have done some indicated homework. His reactions were quick, however.

'He gave me this,' he said, handing over the card which, with everything else to think about, he had forgotten to look at since Counsellor Tan gave it to him last night. Houghton glanced at the card and then exploded with a repertoire of obscenities, delivered more out of excitement than reprobation.

'This Chinese,' he said, stabbing his finger at the card, 'was the Deputy Head of Peking's Mission in Bangkok and a man Dobell was cultivating and had fingered as a potential defector!'

'Well, I didn't know about that,' said Potter defensively. He was staggered by the news. It seemed a few grades higher than the fragmentary and vague reports from French liaison that he had been sending to London during the last few weeks about Palestinian terrorist groups.

'Of course, of course,' said Houghton and picked up the telephone. Then he looked at his watch and slammed the receiver down. 'Lunchtime...' he muttered. He walked round the desk and drew a chair up next to Potter.

'Now tell me, Ian – it is Ian, isn't it?... Tell me about last night... I want to know every nuance!'

*

It is not illegal to walk on the well-kept grass of St James's Park and Ralph Scott-Baker leapt over the two foot high metal palings along the path to make a soft landing; it was a short cut to his office in Carlton House Terrace. On the way, he still had the taste in his mouth of Mrs Houghton's excellent roast-beef sandwiches, but he was also thinking that the husband was a rum fellow. Despite his role as The Supervisor for the last two years, he had never quite got the measure of some of those MI6 officers. The birdwatcher Houghton, for example: it was only in recent months that Houghton had summarily fired one of his junior officers for taking classified material to work on at home. There was no question of sinister motives – the young official was merely hard-pressed and keen. By the book, however, Houghton's draconian penalty was correct.

And yet today, there was Houghton sitting on a park bench with an armful of some of the most sensitive government papers ever to come out of MI6; these documents he had evidently had at home with him because he had admitted going straight to the CISA meetings without calling at the office. The Supervisor was glad that he was only a sort of political advisor with no special concern for security – not to mention morality.

As he walked into a high-ceilinged ante-room en route to his own office, Scott-Baker noticed a visitor sitting at a large table leafing through *The Times*. The Supervisor's Personal Assistant came up quickly and stood between the visitor and Scott-Baker. It was the sort of protective gesture that earns people the title of Personal Assistant. He was half whispering.

'It's Lebedev, the Soviet Minister – he wants to see you urgently.'

'Wants to see *me*?' Scott-Baker said out of the side of his mouth. Over the PA's shoulder he was examining the rather slight, distinguished-looking figure, still engrossed in the top people's daily. 'It's obviously a mistake – didn't you explain…'

'No, he's quite specific, sir.' The PA was conveying earnestness and even urgency with his eyes. Although Scott-Baker had the status of Under-Secretary, his name did not figure in any list normally available to foreign missions, for the simple reason that, as The Supervisor, he had no business with them. He walked across to the table.

'My name is Scott-Baker. What can I do for you, Mr Lebedev?'

The Russian stood up and offered his hand. He was in his mid-fifties, a wiry figure with thin, greying hair and rimless glasses. Well-dressed in a conservative, diplomatic way, the slim form had a considerable presence.

Scott-Baker, in contrast to the other man, looked even more round than usual. His style was different. Almost bald, he was a rather untidy follower of the soft-collar school, but still somehow managing an aura of grace.

And he had a very sharp mind. So finally, it didn't matter how he was dressed. He drew up another chair to the table.

'It's remote from my normal responsibilities,' Lebedev said, 'but I am charged with delivering to the British government information, which we hope will be helpful, concerning Henry Dobell.

'Would you care to come through to my office?' suggested Scott-Baker, his mind racing. He eased off his coat. The Russian shook his head. 'Thank you, but this will only take a few minutes…'

It was now very clear why the Soviet minister had not approached his usual interlocutors at the Foreign Office.

'I will come straight to the point ...' The Russian sounded bored and almost impatient. 'The information is of course reliable. It comes from our ... our responsible authorities: Dobell was kidnapped by Chinese officials late in the evening of 7 March on the outskirts of

Bangkok.'

Scott-Baker drummed his fingers on the table. Fantasies. Nightmares. What had Houghton put in his coffee? He was inclined to ask the Russian for identification. Was this not some form of absurd provocation? A wild KGB effort to discredit the Chinese? Or was this some imposter – a crank roaming the London streets? But nobody was supposed to know that Dobell was even missing. The Supervisor looked hard at the visitor. No, it was indeed Minister Lebedev who took charge of the Soviet Embassy when the Ambassador was away, and Scott-Baker now realised that he had seen him before at receptions.

'Why are you telling us this?'

'Out of a general humanitarian attitude for which the Soviet Union is justly renowned...' said Lebedev blandly.

'Yes, Minister. And there is possibly a further reason...?'

'I am also authorised to say,' continued Lebedev in a matter-of-fact tone, betraying that it was a formula response to an expected question, 'that Dobell has long since been identified as a member of your Secret Intelligence Service... He has studied our country in depth over many years and although we despise his methods and his... er.... situation, we recognise that he is what you would call "an expert on Soviet affairs"—'

'Dobell is a senior diplomat with considerable experience of the Soviet Union and other Eastern European countries,' said Scott-Baker smoothly.

'Well, I hope it will be obvious to you that we have as much interest as you in securing Dobell's release from those Chinese traitors of the revolution.' Lebedev spoke softly and with assurance. The Supervisor understood very well what was meant.

'How did this extraordinary information come to the knowledge of the ... Soviet authorities?' he asked without expecting a proper reply.

'Those responsible in Bangkok had Dobell under observation because of his known criminal activities. It was noted on the night of the 7th, that Dobell's car was forced off the road by a closed van belonging to the Chinese Embassy. He was then driven away in that vehicle.'

In a momentary flash of anger, Scott-Baker slapped his hand on the table.

'If the infamous KGB were watching a cowardly kidnapping, why didn't they intervene?'

Lebedev was too wise, experienced and, essentially, too detached front vulgar Secret Service practices to be much moved by this. He looked at Scott-Baker with a mild, tolerant expression.

'I understand,' he said, 'that on this occasion our resources were too...' The Russian paused, searching for the appropriate word. (Later Scott-Baker and others would learn that that the hesitation had a particular significance.) 'Our resources were too limited.' Lebedev added. 'And in any case, it is not for us to question what goes on in those fields.' With a slight pursing of the mouth, he indicated his indifference and even disdain. He stood up and turned back the copy of *The Times* to page 1.

'It's a good newspaper,' he said. 'Its existence might even be justified if a few more of the population read it...'

He smiled quizzically at The Supervisor, who saw him to the door.

'I should thank you for your cooperation,' Scott-Baker said. 'I assume there will be no formal communication about this...?' It was a rhetorical question. As he shook hands, Lebedev said, 'Believe me, Mr Baker, I find this whole business irregular and distasteful...'

The Supervisor believed him.

*

By 4 p.m. the same afternoon, half a dozen people, gathered in emergency session in Charles Houghton's office, had thrashed out the implications of Potter's news from Paris and the equally remarkable Soviet communication given to Scott-Baker at the Foreign Office. There was general agreement because there was not much choice. Houghton was putting his papers together on the desk and summed it up.

'Approval from upstairs. We get Lawson back on a short-term contract.'

'Don't you think we should at least inform WRU – after all, it's his organisation...' Potter suggested.

'It *was* his organisation,' replied Houghton quickly, 'and for this operation he will be wholly under control of MI6. The Minister has agreed. In fact, I will be looking after Lawson personally...'

Ian Potter glanced across at The Supervisor and half raised an eyebrow; it was only half a reaction. Scott-Baker looked back, blinked twice and dropped his eyes. His was scarcely a reaction at all. But he had something to say. It was almost wishful thinking.

'Why don't you try somebody else on the Chinese – tell them Lawson's unavailable?'

'But Lawson *will* be available,' said Houghton easily. 'Let's do what they want.'

'What makes you so sure he'll agree to come back?' asked The Supervisor. Houghton stood up and surveyed the group, one by one, as he weighed his words.

'Firstly, he will be intrigued and it will touch his vanity to know that we are asking him to come back; then there's the money; his ... gratuity,' Houghton spat the words out, 'was considerable but will not last for ever, and finally it's his simple duty...'

It sounded all right in theory, but Houghton sensed that he had not convinced everybody fully – especially those who had known Lawson.

'I believe, too, that he has a mother living alone in Scotland who has been rather sick recently,' added Houghton casually.

Everything, then, was, decided and the meeting broke up. But at least one participant left wondering just why Charles Houghton had interested himself in the health of Lawson's ailing mother.

Chapter 6

,

Cuernavaca, Mexico

T HE VILLA IS a few miles outside the town itself and away from areas graced by similar residences. The principal two-floor building is a three bed-roomed spread constructed mainly of pale, yellowing stone. On the upper floor, a balcony runs round three sides of the villa. Inside, perhaps the most striking feature is a rather grand, wide staircase with an old wrought-iron handrail which sweeps up from the salon in a ninety-degree arc to the second floor.

It is peaceful, graceful, redolent of unseemly colonial grandeur and the nearest I will ever get to paradise. And my embroidery is advancing well.

The *motif* on my canvas sneak-abouts would be, I decided for reasons of nostalgia, two Chinese characters. The first, on the left foot, gave me no trouble; the Chinese character for 'one' is the same as the English Roman numeral, except that you lay it carefully on its side. With a great sense of artistic balance, I chose for the right upper one of the most complex signs in the Chinese language. This character means variously: (a) anxious, (b) bushy, (c) fragrant herb or (d) a door-god. But what can you expect of a character which requires about thirty separate strokes of the pen or brush to write it?

The great thing is that apart from the no doubt chic and stylish final result, there will be very few people around able to point out that I may have dropped a stitch or two on my right shuffler.

Add to all this the unobtrusive presence of at least

five well-trained and, in the main, grateful Mexican servants – one of whom, Alfredo, arrives on the patio at regular intervals with refills of my sundown Margarita cocktail – and it will be clear that here we have reached the zenith of reactionary indolence and luxury. And I hasten to assure my left-wing friends that it is not even decadent – it's flourishing.

Oh yes, one more thing and by far the most important: as I sit relaxed with my needle-work and habit-forming tequila, rocking gently in a comfortable wicker chair, three yards away, with her long, slim legs propped up slightly and ending on the low balustrade amidst a fine display of delicate white Madagascar Jasmine, reclines Evelyn Los Palamares.

She is writing a letter but every so often smiles across at me or wants to know whether she should bandage my much-spiked thumb, just to ensure that I haven't forgotten she is there. As if that were possible.

And it has been since we were thrown together a summer or two ago (although for a time on opposing sides) in an affair which provoked my premature, but profitable, retirement from HMG's employ. In fact, the Government did very well out of that imaginative operation and my final disposal had official blessing, reluctant though it was. Unofficially, however, I made some powerful and dangerous enemies. But I was now a long way from all that.

No, Evelyn and I are not married. During the initial months when I thought the subject might be brought up in the context of our unlikely but blissful general communion Evelyn never mentioned the word. (And with a lifelong committal to doing nothing irrevocable, it wasn't for me to speak first.) Admittedly, I was baffled by Evelyn's reticence. And finally, through some residual discreet official contacts – old habits die hard – I discovered that Evelyn was partner to a dormant marriage contracted seven years earlier in what can only be described as rigorous circumstances. So that was that. I don't really know whether it suits me or not.

The hacienda is Evelyn's. Her Mexican father died, God bless him, and left it to her. But no money. The upkeep of the place I just about manage from very speculative but so far advantageous investment of my retirement gratuity.

So this is the life. In addition to embellishing my footwear, testing several times a day the pollution level of the swimming pool and unnecessarily pruning the Jungle Flame Ixora shrubs in the driveway, I am - I like to believe - constructively occupied.

I have been writing several hours a day for the past year. In fact, there are a number of more or less complete typescripts which I keep upstairs under the mattress. Those are accounts of sundry episodes in a varied and barely legal career, recorded while still relatively fresh in the memory, rather than left to ferment in an ageing mind to be trotted out in a senile huddle as unlikely after-dinner tales.

A photocopy of the first of these typescripts, which describes how to the disadvantage of a certain foreign government a little less than a quarter of million pounds found its way into a bottom drawer at MI6 Head Office (less an agreed commission that came my way) is lodged with a friendly lawyer in London. In the event of my untimely or violent demise, the typescript would be published, and the lawyer has long since secured a first option from an equally friendly and discerning editor.

This is the only thing between me and the almost certain oblivion that some vindictive spirits in London (not to mention elsewhere) undoubtedly have in mind for me.

Occasionally I sneak off down the road for a day or two at a time to roam around in the massive hills of the Sierra Madre – with memories of that fine Bogart movie of the same name, full of dust, greed and corruption. And when I return to Cuernavaca, footsore and usually none the wiser, the household panders to my various needs in the unlikely belief that they are harbouring a budding, expatriate author.

This is all much, much more than I deserve, as I freely admit in moments of lucidity, but after a year and a half of getting used to it, I am beginning to believe that perhaps I deserve it after all.

Alfredo sidled up again in his baggy white trousers tight at the ankles; this time he didn't bring a glass and his sombrero was hooked over his right hand.

'American visitor coming, Señor Lawson ...'

Evelyn suddenly retrieved her feet from the Madagascar Jasmine and even I stood up. 'Where is he?' I asked. Alfredo gestured with the sombrero. 'Three hundred metres down track, señor.' This is what I mean by the 'well-trained' aspect of our friendly Mexican staff. Evelyn looked at me apprehensively, waiting.

A number of Mexican friends are always calling us, but we haven't seen a real American or European face at the hacienda since we moved in a year ago.

'All right,' I said decisively, 'I'll just nip upstairs and find some cigars.'

'Do you think I should change?' asked Evelyn and plucked at the long, light cotton wrap she was wearing over the bottom bit of a bikini. The white veil was stitched with a simple Mexican design at the edges and it was more or less laced-up just at the waist. Evelyn's long black hair, slung in front over one shoulder, was gathered together by a *rondelle* of yellow Allamanda flowers – culled from our very own backyard, of course. With a good suntan, she looked almost like an Indian squaw – but rather the sort they have in films, schooled in Lausanne for three years and with a recent past in *haute couture*. And in this case, Evelyn had something more than *haute couture* behind her. Yes, this is another of my little excitements – just to see this enchanting figure in her hardly transparent wrap wafting gracefully around, barefoot, on the highly polished red floor-tiles of ex-Papa Palamares' hacienda.

'You're perfect as you are,' I said and went across to kiss her lightly to show I meant it. 'Let this stranger take us as he finds us!'

I then raced upstairs at a pace which visibly upset Alfredo, who was not used to anything moving so quickly in our sleepy neck of the woods.

Suitably hidden on the upper balcony behind come hanging pale mauve blooms of Bengal Clock-vine and window-boxes of some hibiscus thing I've never properly identified, I waited.

From this lookout, you can see the end of the track some three hundred yards away as it dips down to join a road of sorts. On the way up to us, the track curves round behind a ridge and visitors are not visible again until they arrive at the main gates of the short driveway to the villa.

Even then, they are only visible through a ruse; driveways or small alleys leading out onto roads sometimes have a large mirror placed opposite so that oncoming traffic can be seen. We have one of those mirrors, too, but craftily angled so that from a position between the window-boxes on the balcony you can see who it is demanding entry.

I waited. Whoever it was, evidently hadn't the fleetness of foot just demonstrated to Alfredo.

It was dusk and I must have looked away for an instant – upwards, no doubt, at the stars just forming in the gentle Mexican night. Then the bell rang in the house and simultaneously the main-gate-area was lit up,

In the mirror was no American. Huffing and puffing a little, his rather portly form draped in a well-cut, light-grey suit, Charles Houghton stood there, smoothing his upper lip growth with thumb and forefinger.

Chapter 7

MANY IDEAS struck me as I stared at that very worrying (for me) figure from the recent past, the most needling of which was 'Is this the end of the road?' Yet he seemed to be alone.

I walked quietly into the bedroom and unscrewed the broad base of a heavy wooden table-lamp. I slipped the small, nicely balanced automatic into the waistband under my bright red jungle-shirt. Houghton seemed rather elegantly dressed so I quickly wrapped a snappy black foulard round my neck – tied with just the right amount of bounce. Then I lit a long, slim Del Prado cheroot and turned to make a leisurely grand descent at what I hoped would be the right moment.

From the top of the staircase I saw that Evelyn was still discussing something earnestly with the faithful Alfredo. Nobody hurries in Mexico, especially in the country. The bell rang again.

Then I had another thought. Back in the bedroom, I rummaged around in my sock-drawer, found a full magazine case and clipped it into the butt of the automatic. This item is 'nicely balanced' not because my shooting deserves a precision tool, but because, using the blunt end, I can clout – with remarkable effect – various parts of the body which would surprise many a medical practitioner.

That said, I felt that on this occasion, I might actually have to fire it. I looked anxiously at the now loaded pistol in my hand. I wasn't really sure that it still worked. On a sudden impulse I decided to try it. And Houghton might even go away.

From the balcony, I loosed off two rounds into the Mexican night. The result was, dramatic. All the dogs within a mile's radius started barking; our peaceable doves clattered away in panic from the ornamental pigeon loft, and Evelyn came bounding up the stairs to see if I had finally done it.

But at the gates, Houghton – confound it all! – who I could see in the artful mirror, just glanced rather impatiently at his watch, and pressed the bell again.

That settled it. The man had a certain purpose about him and I didn't think that he had come to chase me up for some unpaid VAT.

'I was cleaning it,' I said to my alarmed, beloved Evelyn, breathing heavily at my side. 'Er... why don't you let him in...'

Two minutes later I heard conversation downstairs. First some bass, dulcet tones:

'Mrs. Lawson?... My name is Houghton... Charles... Yes, Charles. I am sorry to arrive unannounced—'

'How do you do... You want to see Ken of course... Come and sit down. He's upstairs—'

'Yes, I know – I heard him.'

By which time, I was unhurriedly stepping down from above, one hand sliding along the finely worked iron stair-rail and the other fondling a quality cigarillo. A weekend Omar Sharif without the moustache and not nearly so good at bridge.

I will say this for him: for most of the time Houghton was smooth, civil and almost conciliatory and he smiled – laughed even – at the right moments. It was an impressive performance of self-control. And confidence. But every so often I could sense his suppressed fury accumulating as he gradually hoisted in various aspects of our flower-filled hacienda life. When Evelyn leaned forward in front of him to offer Mexican titbits – garnishing for our dinner later – I noticed that his eyes were not merely counting the ice-cubes in his tall whisky glass.

Evelyn left us on some pretext and I listened politely while Houghton related some ridiculous story about the Chinese wanting to talk to me about the abduction of one Henry Dobell, an old friend of mine - not a close one, but certainly a friend. I honestly thought Houghton's work was getting on top of him and that he had gone a little mad. Then I played with the idea that Houghton's condition was even worse than appeared. Perhaps it was some wild scheme of his to get me back home where he would be in a better position to indulge his ambition to have me impaled on the railings outside the WRU premises as a warning to others.

But as Houghton added more and more convincing and corroborative detail to the background and started talking about a 'short-term contract' and 'remuneration', it seemed to me that it was all too unlikely to be a ruse; if Houghton wanted to trick me into going back to the UK he would have chosen a less fanciful scenario. I concluded, therefore, that the situation described by Houghton – astonishing though it was – was real. I was just seeking clarification of the financial aspects when the doorbell rang again.

Evelyn reappeared under the archway at the entrance to the salon and said uncertainly to me, 'It's Lorenzo…'

A *coup de théâtre* if ever there was one! This would add a final touch of charm to the evening. 'Show him in, show him in!' I said, trying to keep the ecstasy from my voice.

A small man smiling broadly and dressed in a very expensive raw-silk suit came towards us with both hands outstretched – one towards we and the other towards the glass of straight tequila that Evelyn was offering. After effusive greetings, he recoiled apologetically a bit at the sight of Houghton standing grimly to one side.

'Charles, let me introduce Commissioner Lorenzo Bravo y Magnana – he's the Chief of Police... Charles Houghton, an old friend of mine from London.'

For the first time that evening, Houghton's assured manner faltered. As he shook hands, he had that bleak look of someone improperly equipped for unexpected obstacles. But he recovered quickly. He was resilient, that man. And for the few minutes Lorenzo was with us, Anglo-Saxon poise reigned.

After some casual domestic chatter and a second tequila, the Mexican prepared to leave. He apologised for 'intruding', said that he had not known that we had company and declined to stay for dinner as he had been invited up from Mexico City to dine elsewhere in Cuernavaca that evening. He claimed to have been 'delighted' to have met Señor Houghton, shook his hand again and told me to stay with my guest.

Half moving away, he kissed Evelyn warmly on both checks and then patted her bottom affectionately. Houghton gaped and turned to me. 'It's her uncle,' I said.

Under the archway, Lorenzo called over his shoulder, 'Ken, I see you at the fiesta next week, right?'

I excused myself to friend Charles and exchanged places with Evelyn. On the way out Lorenzo had his arm draped over my shoulder, so I asked a small favour.

'When he leaves here, you couldn't make sure that he knows he's being followed, could you?'

'He knows already,' Lorenzo smiled at me. 'They flashed his passport details to me at Headquarters...'

While I was thinking that over, Lorenzo still protecting me with one arm from the uncertainties of the Mexican night, with his other hand delved between my shirt buttons with a snakelike thrust. He weighed the automatic in his hand. Walking with me towards the main gates of the villa, Lorenzo said sternly: 'You are not allowed to have this, Ken .... And also you don't have a licence for your two sporting rifles, You fill out a form soon, please.'

He pinched my cheek with one hand and gave me back the pistol with the other. 'I think I don't see you at the fiesta next week, right?'

When I came back, Houghton was examining with exaggerated attention a jade ring that Evelyn wears on her left hand. He watched her carefully as she tactfully slid off to the kitchen area.

'Money?' I said mildly, being greatly encouraged by the recent unexpected show of local reinforcements.

'Five thousand pounds for a three-month contract but we expect the business to be settled well within the period...' said Houghton efficiently.

'I want half in cash before I leave Mexico,' I said. Houghton swung open his well-tailored lightweight worsted jacket while I looked hard. He pulled out from an inner pocket a buff-coloured envelope and placed it on the inlaid enamel Chinese table separating us.

'There's £500 in tenners as a retainer,' he said in a non-negotiable way.

'That's not nearly enough! And what about my travel?'

Another easy movement of the hand and Houghton

passed me an air-line ticket. I examined it.

'It's only one-way,' I said.

'It's first-class,' he countered.

'I won't go without a return ticket!' I exclaimed. 'After all...' I added, waving my arm around at the priceless hacienda. Houghton looked at me coldly and fingered his moustache. Then he snorted impatiently and began counting out more notes from another wad. As he continued with this encouraging exercise, I had an idea: 'I will have to buy some winter clothes, you realise...'

He stopped dead and for a moment I really believed that I was pressing my luck. But he finally slammed the rest of what must have been a total of some £2500 retainer fee on the table; then he very carefully handed me a receipt to sign.

'That's fine,' I murmured and, all poised to account for this largesse, I looked up and said: 'What name should I use?'

He stood up suddenly and there was unbridled hate in his eyes. By some happy chance Evelyn rejoined us at that moment to ask if Charles would be staying, for a meal –'*manchamanteles, chile rellenos* and *jalisco pozole*' (beautifully pronounced) for a start. Graciously 'No thank-you' because his embassy driver was waiting at the bottom of the track to take the popular Houghton back to Mexico City, where he was invited to dinner.

'Your driver is actually drinking beer with our gardener,' I said. 'We had him bring the car up – it's a long walk down there.'

'We'll see you in London then in forty-eight hours, Ken...' said Houghton, looking at Evelyn.

'Right,' I said and I didn't dare look at anybody.

Charles Houghton bid us all a perfunctory thanks and

goodnight, and left.

As we walked back along the driveway, I paused and noted some shuffling movement on the edges of the dove-cot. How do they manage to come back home – these birds – in the dark?

Evelyn slipped her hand into mine; after one and a half years this still sends me tingling, into wonderland.

'You fool around too much, Ken – that man is dangerous... I saw it in his eyes.'

'Not only his eyes, *mi corazón*: in the hand-stitched lining pocket of his sexy worsted he carries a long snout .22, and even if he does pant a bit uphill, he knows how to use it.'

'Then why for God's sake are you getting into this!' Evelyn swung round and blocked my advance towards the arousing smells of a Mexican dinner.

'For a start,' I said, 'I'm intrigued – I've never heard such a story; and then I'm a bit flattered that the mob should ask for my services – vanity, no doubt; next, the money is important, you won't deny that ...'

Evelyn didn't move. She stood there under the stone archway leading to the salon with hands on hips in an attitude of defiance.

'Of course, I still have a British passport... It's my simple duty.'

'Nonsense!'

I looked round, but happily Houghton had gone of course. We sat down by the small Chinese table and suddenly there were Mexicans everywhere handing us drinks.

'And another thing,' I said, 'Henry Dobell is an old cobber of mine and, well, frankly, it annoys me to think that he has been carted off by the Chinese.'

'When did you know Dobell?' Evelyn asked suspiciously.

'You've been listening at keyholes again,' I said, 'but if you must know, Henry and I in the early days were on a course together, learning how to dynamite trains…'

Evelyn suddenly threw her arms in the air, made a contemptuous noise and the bottom half of her cotton wrap fell all over the pace. I looked, sighed and returned to the argument.

'… and in off periods when they ran out of trains, Henry made me listen to a lot of advanced music which I didn't like and taught me to play chess – which I took to in an amateur way.'

'I don't believe you dynamited *any* trains!' exclaimed Evelyn, pointing a jade-laden finger at me.

'*Never mind!*' I shouted. 'Uncle Henry is currently at the tender mercies of the anti-Confucius brigade – your erstwhile sworn enemies!' In turn, I pointed accusingly at the light of my life. '... And it seems I am in a position to do something about it!'

'Dinner is served ...' said a cautious voice some yards away.

'In any case, with all your tricky questions – whose side are you *on*?' That did it and we settled round the dining table on the patio.

After dinner, when the hubbub had died away, Evelyn left me in no doubt which side she was on.

Chapter 8

Bangkok

THE PAN AM BOEING heaved and lurched down through flocculent tufts of grey and white cumulous and suddenly below us stretched the very flat Thai landscape laid out in shades of green, some vivid, others soft and sombre. The patchwork of rice-paddies, coconut plantations and tapioca was knitted together by gleaming silver strips of irrigation ditches, which became murky brown as the plane dropped another thousand feet or two.

On the ground, swinging round at the end of the runway, there was a delay; Pan Am's reassuring wizard at the front end of the aircraft addressed us for the last time.

He was the one who had actually got us off the ground at Heathrow. That had been a moment to remember 'We gotta full load here, folks,' he drawled, 'don't be alarmed if we seem a bit long on the take-off run... Sit back, enjoy yourselves... Okay – we're rollin'.' So we had thundered down the strip for an age. And then an hour later; with the aircraft bouncing about in the elements at 25,000 feet (what were the elements *doing* here at 25,000 feet anyway?) 'Uh… this is your Captain speaking... bit of unexpected turbulence here ... uh, we'll be waitin' on dinner a bit until we're through it...'. Then somewhere over the Middle East he was 'Jes takin' this ole bird up another 5,000 feet... uh... due to... uh... some unscheduled traffic below us...' Everybody had peered down and there was a full-scale unpublished dogfight

63

going on between Syrian MIGs and Israeli Phantoms.

A few other relaxed, comforting interventions from the cockpit during the flight and then, on the ground, at Bangkok, a farewell message: 'Uh ... a minute or two delay here. We're making way for some military traffic... uh... well, been nice having you folks aboard. Hope you enjoyed the flight... uh... Thank you.'

Thank *you*, too! Wouldn't we all be only too glad for pilots to he paid whatever salary they want as long as they can guarantee to keep these machines in the air for the appropriate length of time? Let them have medals and extra long holidays as well if it means we're sure of getting there!

We politely followed a sleek-looking Royal Thai Airforce FSA, screaming along the centre-line of the tarmac. It was painted very dark green all ever but the nose was adorned with a lurid yellow tiger. The fighter peeled off and the pilot leapt out – also all insignia and dash – and was driven away in a waiting jeep.

At the hatchway, the heat hit me with a moist thump, and I suddenly thought that I should have asked Charles Houghton for an extra tropical clothing allowance – as well.

Houghton had objected to me coming to Bangkok. His attitude seemed to be based on something other than the extra expense. My argument had been that the investigator always visits the scene of the crime. Houghton acidly pointed out that I was no sort of 'investigator' and that my job was just to present myself to the Chinese, Counsellor Tan, in Paris as requested. I countered this by claiming that I could not conduct myself confidently in Paris without some personal examination of the circumstances of Dobell's abduction in Bangkok. A surprising number in committee agreed with this and Houghton gave in with bad grace to a majority vote. But he had the last word: 'The fleshpots of Bangkok are not, I understand, what they used to be.'

I had spent less than forty-eight hours in London being briefed and under Houghton's tight control. Even 'the first 'evening' was arranged – ostensibly some relaxing entertainment paid for by Head Office. First an excellent dinner in the nevertheless curiously phoney atmosphere of one of the 'in' restaurants in Kings Road, SW3 at which Houghton was present. He excused himself after dinner from the group of five and one other left with him. The two who remained then took me to a private 'club' where, finally, I was left in the company of a youngish bulldog in Houghton's Directorate who had his hands full with a moonlighting Swedish au pair; I was the subject of particular attention from a neat brunette who was a cut above the average – and in some of these places, he average is dazzling.

I don't know whether she also temporarily belonged to Houghton's Directorate nor what he expected, but at 1 a.m. I had had enough and announced gracefully that I was going to bed. The bulldog looked at me desperately:

'Oh, come on, Ken, the night's young...'

'Stay a while,' I said. 'Don't worry – I'll tell Director Charles you drove me back to the hotel...'

The following day, before being taken to Heathrow, I did manage to evade supervision for a lunchtime haircut, and who should be in the Curzon Street barber's shop at the same time but Phillip Goodenough from WRU. No, this is not a happy textual coincidence; he had been there by careful arrangement because Boris, as he is affectionately called, is a good friend, knows a thing or two about Russians and passed on a few points as we reclined in adjacent operating chairs.

Normally barbers are chatty fellows. As Boris droned on, using disguised language and ridiculous euphemisms, our two artists became as deaf-mutes. But they did a stylish, unhurried job and were grateful for the generous tips.

Back to a sultry afternoon in Thailand. At the Immigration desk a Thai official in shirt-sleeves, with epaulettes that strangely resembled those of a British RN lieutenant, asked for my passport. In pulling it out, I also found in my hand an envelope given to me across the table at the end of the last group session by Ralph Scott-Baker, the F.O. liaison man. Ralph Baker was not quite a friend of mine, but he belonged to that fringe group of acquaintances that everyone has, who probably would be counted as friends if the circumstances were right. He had casually asked if I would mind awfully giving this note to Reggie somebody in the Embassy if I saw him. It was something about an unpaid bill at the Bath Club. A pleasure, of course. I had pocketed the envelope and had forgotten about it until now.

'How long are you staying in Thailand, sir?' I looked, vaguely surprised, at the envelope, which was not addressed to Reggie somebody, but simply to 'Ken'.

'How long are you staying, please?' It was an impatient tone. The chop was poised over my brand-new passport. I glanced up quickly. 'Sorry – just a few days…' Thump. Next please.

'You're in transit, madam – please join the others over there...' I wouldn't have his job for all the world.

Once through the barrier and out into the main hall, I stopped and tore open the note. 'No chance to see you alone, Take my advice – tread very softly. I smell vengeance in the air. Enjoy Bangkok. R.'

All I can say is that it was a good job I had not opened this note, say, just as Hank, the deep South pilot, was advising us that today we would be a very long time careering down the Heathrow runway to get airborne. I continued to stare unnecessarily at the message, feeling in part alarmed but the rest of it was cold anger.

'Mr Lawson?' A young Englishman in a Persil-white short-sleeved shirt and a distinguished tie was elbowing his way through a crowd of welcomers – genuine friends and relatives, hotel touts, minibus drivers, taxi owners and a leavening of the sort of people who are always at the arrival gates of airports for no apparent purpose.

''fraid not,' I said. 'My name's Campbell.' He was asking the same question of some of my fellow travellers behind as I went out to the parking area. The Embassy car was there, unattended, in a privileged position just outside. It was a Rover 3500 – good heavens! – was it even Dobell's vehicle being recycled for airport trips?

Amidst a chorus of entreaties to take this or that standard taxi or limousine with air-conditioning, I eventually found a 'samlor' – an open motorised tricycle (plus driver) with a canvas top at the passenger end – which would putter into the city centre. The samlor is uncomfortable for a weary traveller and it is slow, but it is a nice, cool, way to move in Bangkok. True, I could have taken an air-conditioned taxi or even the luxury Rover, but I didn't feel up to making polite conversation with a young Old Harrovian. Besides, I did not wish to accommodate Houghton's evident desire for me to be under the official eye twenty-four hours a day. Ralph Baker's friendly note only reinforced my fine spirit of independence.

Halfway along the seventeen-mile highway that leads from Don Muang airport to the outskirts of Bangkok, the Rover hissed by us at breakneck speed, and its young, fair-haired driver was no doubt desperately wrestling with ideas to excuse his arrival at the Embassy empty-handed.

As the samlor bumped and creaked into the centre, I felt a certain nostalgia. Those pleasurable first few moments during which the smells and sounds of an Asian city revisited have their full impact. You don't get that in an air-conditioned Rover.

Bangkok is a popular port of call for travellers heading for the perhaps more simple tourist attractions of Hong Kong or Tokyo; a few days stopover is a common formula – time enough to buy a yard or two of Thai silk and try the fiercely hot local curry. Gemstones, too, are generally thought to be a bargain here. But the wary will decide for themselves whether that emerald in the Chinese jeweller's display counter is natural, or merely an artifice of Dr Chatham. After all, this is also the land of the Emerald Buddha reposing in a Bangkok temple and who really knows if that fabulous seventeen-inch high statuette at the top of its tiered golden pyramid is carved in emerald or not? From about fifteen feet away, which is the nearest point usually accessible to mortal viewers, it looks more like a jade or serpentine.

The '*putta-putta*' noise was now accompanied by clouds of blue smoke from the well-worn engine as the samlor stopped. Not at the Temple of the Emerald Buddha, but in the driveway of the British Embassy where there is little sightseeing to be done and which is not on anybody's tourist route. A not quite elegant two-storied, barrack-like structure set in not quite well-cared for grounds, with the Ambassador's residence tucked away at the rear. In the Chancery forecourt, I noticed the Rover being given a leisurely wash by one of the Embassy's Thai minions.

I walked round to a back entrance – and even in these hair-raising days nobody bothered to stop me – down a corridor or two, being bidden 'good afternoon' by sundry inhabitants, up some stairs and finally arriving at an unmarked door which didn't open when I tried it. There was a bell-push to the side. I didn't hear it ring, but within two seconds a six-inch square view-hole with a metal grill in the middle of the door slid back and half a face looked at me.

'My name is Lawson. I want to see the Manager,' I said. What the rest of the face was doing I didn't know but the visible part successfully conveyed stony indifference. A slight hesitation, then: 'Just a moment, please.' As the trapdoor closed I pressed the bell immediately and the view hole snapped open again to reveal the same pale blue eyes expressing as much interest as the first time round. 'He's expecting me...' I added, with a confidential wink. Click. Isolation again.

While I stared at this somehow hostile door, I became aware of a long shadow which had spread over most of the immediate surrounds. I turned slowly and suddenly there seemed to be a lot of turbulence about again.

'You're late,' I said. 'What kept you?'

'I arrived yesterday on a special flight…' replied MI6's Ian Potter very easily. 'Please…' He made a polite ushering movement... 'Shall we go in?' He slid past me with a solid mortise lock key at the ready.

My God, he was light on his feet for a man that big.

Chapter 9

SPREAD AROUND on a desk in a side office were sundry files, two empty coffee cups and, by now, a full ashtray. An ill-fitting air-conditioner in one window juddered and coughed in regular cycles as if someone was feeding it every five minutes with thick cardboard to shred. Potter was stretched back in a chair, tapping his fingertips together and staring at his feet a long way away. I was leafing glumly through a file for the third time; it was a record of Henry Dobell's known movements during the days preceding his abduction.

One of his last official appointments had been to meet a Lao agent at the Cathay Hotel; after that he had some routine meetings here at the Embassy and some purely social engagements. He had been to see his American colleague once and returned to the office in good humour, retailing a couple of White House scandal jokes. The following evening he disappeared. There was little else that was relevant on file here; the main point – that Dobell was in Chinese hands – had been established from the revelations elsewhere, not Bangkok. So my 'scene of the crime' investigations up till now seemed as futile as Charles Houghton had said they would be.

Potter was fed up because, having studied the papers already, he had come to the same conclusion. He was also annoyed because I told him that I didn't believe Houghton had sent him to Bangkok to be likewise 'briefed' but rather that he was there to keep an eye on me. Potter had snorted 'Ridiculous' and had grumbled something about my 'persecution complex', but he looked very thoughtful at the time.

'You must be tired after the flight,' Potter suggested reasonably. 'I'll run you to the hotel.'

It was true: nothing would have suited me better than to slip between the sheets for a few hours – especially after all that nervous exhaustion of an extra full load and too much gravity at Heathrow, buffeting and not enough gravity at high altitude, diversions because of somebody's war down below, to say nothing of 'the biggest electrical storm' the navigator had ever seen – 'it filled the whole radar screen'. (I had crept up behind the crew's refreshment table in the transit lounge at Karachi to listen to these confidences). Yes, I was tired.

'Certainly not,' I told Potter. 'I slept like a log since London only to be woken for feeding... I want to see the Thai Liaison report on movements of Soviet personnel during the week in question.' It wasn't even certain that such a report existed. But it would be a normal handout in a country where the locals are supposed to be friendly.

'What the devil do you want that for?' said Potter crossly.

'Clues...'

Potter looked at me with a flicker of an idea in his eyes. I lit another cigarette while he picked up the intercom to ask for the paper. For no doubt highly valid 'need-to-know' reasons, I was being kept out of the main office and I was being handled entirely by the ubiquitous Potter from Paris in an adjoining 'visitors room'. I stubbed the cigarette out after two puffs when I realised that I was into the second packet in twenty-four hours.

'Whose is that?' I asked, indicating some scuba-diving equipment stacked in a corner.

'Henry's,' said Potter. 'He is very keen apparently – goes off most weekends.' Dobell knew what he was doing when he asked for a posting in Thailand.

The young fair-haired fellow with the telling tie came in with a few sheets of printed foolscap. He looked at me unpleasantly.

'I thought you said your name was Campbell,' he said with too much sarcasm for it really to be effective.

'What does the report say?' I asked.

He shot a surprised glance at the document in his hand. 'I don't know, I haven't read it... It's of no interest to us here...' He hesitated. '... We just copy these things to the Security Service. It sometimes helps to keep them up to date on Russian operating methods.' He paused and his very clean-shaven chin came forward a little defiantly.

'And by the way ...' He was going to make his point, this young man, '... I don't appreciate driving all the way to the airport on a fool's errand. I'm rather busy, you know...'

It was mostly the pompous tone that grated. Out of the corner of my eye I saw that even Potter had winced.

'Yes, it's very hard when you're busy...' I nodded sympathetically. '... It perhaps explains why, even though you were told the KGB had been watching Henry – your own Section Chief – you didn't have time to read what the Thais had to say about local Russian movements during the period...'

The chin retreated, dropped a little and his mouth hung open. Then his fair skin coloured and he slammed the papers on the desk. Potter, in one lithe movement, gathered his great length together and sprang up. He was not somebody to be in the way of when he unwound like that.

'All right, Harvey – leave us to it!'

Harvey? I wondered which end of the name that belonged to. 'Thank you, Harvey,' I said as the door slammed.

We sat there, Potter and I, studying this mundane document for five minutes or so. There were some intriguing titbits: the Soviet First Secretary had called at two rather special massage parlours during the week and the Ambassador's wife had sacked the seventh cook in two months; a member of the Cultural Section had become very drunk in Patpong Road one night after attending a Thai boxing match and the Embassy radio operator, from his shopping round town, was evidently building his own hi-fi ensemble. Other trivia included standard accounts of officials going to receptions and being otherwise involved in legitimate business. Conspicuous by its absence was any record of contact between Soviet diplomats and the Thai Ministry of Foreign Affairs. A few odd displacements on the part of some officials probably indicated Intelligence activity but none of it seemed relevant to Dobell. Of course, these reports were fragmentary, because the Russians are as good as anybody (and better than most) in disguising their clandestine activity.

However, on the last page was an appendix describing a perfectly ordinary minor 'incident' in the parking lot of a downtown cinema. It was a Thai Police account in contrast with the rest which came from the Security agencies. After one evening show when *patrons* were collecting their transport, one vehicle belonging to the Soviet Embassy had backed into and just touched another car. There had been no visible damage, but as the Thai policemen came up (they were merely on the scene directing traffic) the drivers of the two cars seemed to be having a stand-up argument. One was Alexander Karpov, an official at the Soviet Embassy and the other was a German woman not further identified in the account. Karpov's name had cropped up before, and he had already been mentioned in the report in the context of 'probable Intelligence activity'.

'Let's just find out who this German woman was,' I suggested. Potter made a 'why bother?' gesture but he went into the main office to telephone Police HQ.

It had occurred to me that Intelligence Officers do not usually like to row in public places – especially if there's virtually nothing to row about. People so employed have a heavy conscience and are constrained to be retiring creatures when there's a risk of publicity. I was also reminded of a phrase used several times by the Russian expert Boris in the Curzon Street barber's chair – 'elaborate contacting procedures'.

Potter came back and his face had brightened. He handed me a slip of paper which read: 'Christel Scholze, aged 32, West German passport No. 342197, archaeologist Bremen Institute, on 3 months tourist visa, *and*, address in Bangkok: Cathay House Hotel room 301!'

'Hmm…' Potter slid back to his near horizontal position in the chair. 'It's probably coincidence ... odd though,' he mused.

The door burst open and the fair young man came in at the trot, his face a little flushed with excitement.

'I say – the *fraulein* at the Cathay – do you realise Henry was using that hotel!'

With a hand hiding my eyes, I glanced sideways at Potter. Tapping his fingertips together again, he looked impassively through his big-framed glasses at fresh, bouncing Harvey. Potter and I, momentarily joined in a common reaction, just stared at Harvey without a word until the latter became uncomfortable and left abruptly. There was an aspect to Potter that I was beginning to appreciate greatly.

'I'm going to have a look around the hotel,' I said, standing up.

'I'll come with you,' volunteered the Potter as if he meant it.

'No!' I said sharply, before he had time to pull it all together. 'Er ... in this town of happy little people, you're too conspicuous!' It was said in a conciliatory tone but Potter still drew one leg back from the centre of the room to point nearer his chair. He didn't quite believe me.

'You stay here,' I said. 'If I disappear, too, you might be needed.'

Chapter 10

AT 6 P.M. THERE WAS quite a throng milling round the reception desk of the Cathay House Hotel: a group of impatient new arrivals, people of all nationalities carrying newspapers and slim briefcases, returning from meetings and conferences, and a few tourists. The reception clerk was occupied handing over room keys, so I tapped discreetly on the glass panelling of the cashier's office.

'They're busy at the front desk – perhaps you can help me... I was supposed to meet one of your hotel guests here a week or more ago. I was delayed and have only just arrived in Bangkok.....   I just wonder if he left a forwarding address – his name is Wiley, Mr N. Wiley...' This was the name Dobell used at the hotel and what I wanted to find through this indirect enquiry was which room he had used.

The twenty-five-year-old, neat European – presumably a trainee 'manager' of sorts – left us with a cheerful 'Certainly, sir...' He was back in a few seconds with a typed index card.

'Mr N. Wiley from New Zealand?'

'That's him.'

'Well, you're not too late, sir – he's still here – room 304.' The dapper young man, who was certainly bound for extra rapid promotion, smiled agreeably – happy to be able to pass on the good news.

'I beg your pardon?' I said.

'Mr Wiley is still is at the hotel, sir.... er...' he glanced at the index card again, '... in fact his room is paid for until the end of the month.' He smiled again, flashed his hands in a gesture of clerical blessing and slumped down behind columns of figures.

Some surprises in life are so complete that at first they just bounce off the mind; the fact may register like an item of weather news, but the import doesn't sink in.

Almost automatically, I went again to the reception desk surrounded by a small crowd seeking attention of one sort or another and looked carefully along the rows of pigeon holes at the rear. Box 304 was complete with key. It was pointless but I used the house 'phone to call Dobell's room. There was naturally no reply.

Without thinking further about the absurd proposition that Dobell was still at the hotel, I went back and joined the queue at the desk. The key to room 301, belonging to the German archaeologist, was also hanging in its place. I made the right guess and inserted myself between two guests who were merely collecting keys. What's one more at rush hour? '301, please…' Slap on the counter and the Thai clerk was already looking enquiringly at the next customer.

I didn't have time for subtleties or precautions; I was due to leave for Paris the following day and there were certain questions to be answered first. After a Russian admission that Dobell had been under surveillance, we had discovered a probable Soviet I.O. Karpov, in contact – publicly though it had been (already a theory was forming about this) - with a 'German' woman who just happened to be staying practically next door to Dobell in the same hotel. All coincidence? I didn't believe it.

I chose to walk up to the third floor rather than take the lift: to familiarise myself with some terrain in case I had to run somewhere.

Room 301 was minimum-rate standard twin

accommodation with bathroom – comfortable but nothing luxurious. Having closed the door behind me and pressed the 'safety' stud, I went to the window and looked for an escape route. The full-length window slid open onto a tiny balcony with a wave of warm, humid air, which somehow seemed a lot more healthy than the dry, refrigerated sort being piped into the room from a grill high in the wall.

The next balcony was some four feet away. Yes, I know, on television or cinema screens actors – or, more likely, stuntmen - they take small gaps like that in their stride. A hundred feet or so below was the hard asphalt of the parking lot. Heights make me dizzy. I closed the window again. It would take very obvious mortal danger within before I went leaping around outside.

I kicked off my shoes and pulled a pillow out from under the bedcover; my one item of luggage – a zip-up leather bag – I placed conspicuously on the floor so that it would be the first thing seen by anyone coming into the room.

It was a tidy room and there were very few personal belongings lying around; a pair of fluffy slippers I pushed further under the bed out of sight and I threw my coat over a chair on which were stacked other female bits and pieces, including a nicely wrapped package of returned laundry.

The chest of drawers revealed nothing but clothing, some items of which surprised us, but there was no time for speculation.

The built-in wardrobe had a sliding door and it was locked. With a bottle-opener I found in the bathroom, I prised the thing open. The wood splintered, some screws fell to the floor and the feeble metal catch bent out of shape. Lawson, the delicate-fingered Raffles of the Orient. But this wasn't the moment for refinements.

A lightweight raincoat and suede jacket, together with some other garments, were hanging in the closet by the door. At the back, pushed away on the floor in a corner were a paper carrier bag marked 'New Thai Store, Silom Road, Bangkok' and a leather-cased object the size and shape of Kellogg's super-economy packet. The latter I dragged out onto the carpet and squatted down. Every so often, from the less than quarter-inch crack at the bottom of the door, shadows passed, sometimes accompanied by voices, as guests went by in the corridor outside.

The leather casing had a strange look about it to a suspicious eye because it lacked any 'commercial' finish. One side unbuttoned to reveal the deck of a tape-recorder. It was a joyful moment. The control panel of the machine merely had numbers and gradations, without usual informative markings like 'Volume Control' or 'Tone'. The absence of the proud manufacturer's name was also a giveaway. Very clearly it was an apparatus tooled-up in a special government workshop. And I had a good idea about which government that was.

While still gleefully studying the tell-tale panel, out of the corner of my eye I became aware of a shadow under the door which wasn't passing. I never have much luck on these occasions and fully expected the door to be flung open and there would be Lawson caught, in no uncertain way, with his fingers in the cookie-jar.

I bundled the leather top in place and pushed the recorder back into the cupboard. While I was about it, I noticed that the carrier bag contained an ornamental ashtray – a rather ungainly bowl of orange plastic.

Small, soft sounds of the door-handle being tried made me start and I stared at the half my side of the door. It was moving very slightly. The shadow danced and a woman's voice called out: 'Excuse me, I seem to have locked myself out. Could you find me a spare key, please…' The voice, I thought, had a slight German accent. 'Yes, ma'm...' replied a Thai room-maid from further along the corridor.

I slid over to the bed and arranged myself in exhausted repose but in such a way that I could see the door reflected in the dressing-table mirror. It was only a matter of seconds before a short rachetting noise announced the pass-key in the lock. The door opened and through half-closed eyes I had my first view of Fraulein Christel Scholze. But never mind that for the moment – where was the Thai maid on whose presence I was counting to absorb or deflect any real difficulty?

The door was still open but there were no retainers in the wake of Fraulein Scholze who had seen fit to make a solo entry. I didn't like this at all. About five feet eight inches of thirty-year-old blonde, hair kept in place by a band over the crown, wearing a shortish beige Thai cotton dress and long, good – perhaps a trifle muscular – tanned legs standing in those canvas-topped clogs which seem to be all the rage. She wasn't exactly my idea of a German archaeologist.

Already excited by the discoveries in the room, my heart began to pound in earnest. No, not because of the tall blonde aspect (other fellows, I know, would be revelling in it) but because this female allegedly German academic was sufficiently sure of herself to tackle the situation without help from the hotel management. And when she quietly closed the door, not taking her eyes off me, I rather wished I had Potter hiding in the bathroom to give me a hand.

The slight noise of the door closing was my cue to turn over with a sleepy grunt. Fraulein Scholze stood there very still, her left hand holding a strap of her shoulder bag and the other resting on the top of the open bag itself.

I opened my eyes, blinked unseeingly and then, feigning startled awareness of her presence, I sat up quickly on the bed, rubbing my eyes.

'What time is it?' I said.

Chapter 11

FRAULEIN SCHOLZE didn't bother to tell me what the time was.

'What are you doing in my room?' It was a flat, rather careful enquiry with nothing unnerved or scandalised about it. I felt very uneasy indeed. I looked at her in wide-eyed amazement and slid my stockinged feet to the carpet.

'Now look here,' I said indignantly. 'This is *my* room – I've just arrived after a long flight and *I'm tired!'*

When caught with your pants down, move to the attack. Or if that doesn't sound quite as I meant it, consider that in France, where it's a fine art, the driver who hits another vehicle, which is stationary at the time, will argue vehemently, call drunken witnesses from cafés, vilify innocent bystanders and hurl insults at the other fellow to insist that the latter is in the wrong.

Blonde Christel Scholze glanced at my zip-up bag in the middle of the floor with its airline labels prominently showing. Yes, sometimes I do manage to get it right.

'Oh ...' For a second she looked confused and had even half-turned to make an apologetic exit. Then reason asserted itself and she returned to the charge, but there was a note of negotiation in her voice.

'I have been here for the last month. My things are here...' she said, pushing open the bathroom door with a nice flick of a brown, trim ankle.

I tried to look surprised and irritated. 'What's wrong with those people,' I grumbled, moving across to the table to pick up the key. 'Here – you look at this: THREE-O-ONE!'

I stared silently around me as if in the dawn of a great comprehension. Now or never. 'Well, I'm terribly sorry – they were busy at the Front Desk and obviously gave me the wrong key... I just came in and flopped down.'

I looked at Fraulein Scholze, smiled a little – embarrassed and properly contrite. I smoothed over the bedcover, put on my shoes and murmuring more apologies prepared to leave. I slung ny coat on my arm, dropping the key in a pocket, and headed towards fair Christel by the door.

'You can leave the key behind...' It was said tolerantly but without much humour. More distraught apologies.

Even then I thought I had got away with it. She moved back a step as if to open the door and let me pass. But my later guess was that she had noticed, without commenting on it, the mutilated lock to the wardrobe-closet.

As I bumbled level with her, one clog caught me behind the right knee and the leg just seemed to disappear. Sinking, off-balance, I was set up to receive the other heavy piece of fashion footwear, which smashed into my left leg an inch below the kneecap. In retrospect, her timing was perfect.

I just crumbled to the carpet with the pain blotting out any kind of response; it felt as if my leg was shattered in a hundred places. Then I was aware of my jacket being pulled back halfway down my arms and an expert hand flicking about here and there.

'Move over by the deck – but stay on the floor!'

I looked up into the snout of a nasty little automatic, but it didn't have a muffler – which was something. Two very brown ankles kept pace with me as I heaved myself along the carpet in the direction required.

Stay on the floor? With no usable legs, it was either a superfluous or sadistic instruction – or both. On the way to the allotted resting place, I had to stop my humiliating crawl. The pain in my left leg was unbelievable and I retched drily. Looking ahead, panting and groaning. I noted some shaft of light laying on a smooth calf, which picked out the sparse, very fine down not usually visible. A small bonus for good triers.

Where the devil was Potter? She couldn't kick *him* about like this. Or perhaps she could.

'Stay there!'

I stopped, gratefully, and became aware that the leg which I thought had gone was still there; it was now throbbing with pins and needles. I tried to collect myself, ignoring the pain in my other leg.

'Don't move any more!' Still waving the pistol at me, Fraulein Scholze backed towards the telephone on the bedside table.

'Good idea,' I moaned. 'I want to have a word with the manager myself.' She had picked up the receiver and I knew that she wasn't about to call anybody on the hotel staff.

Now, to shoot somebody in cold blood requires a great deal of motivation unless the performer is manifestly unbalanced. There was nothing 'unbalanced' about this young woman as far as I could see and moreover, whatever her motivation, she was unlikely actually to fire that gun in a room of a busy hotel; these things make a distinctive noise and complications set in. However, I did consider that whoever this fit and well-trained blonde was about to contact might arrive in no time with a few other ideas on how to dispose of the intruder.

So thinking, *in extremis*, I launched myself on my one partially functioning leg at this striking figure, in what is fondly known in some circles as 'a rugger tackle'.

A great crash and another very unpleasant wrench of something in my shoulder signalled that I had arrived at the bedside locker. But at least I had my hands around her ankles. Simultaneously with my desperate yanking, she held the pistol in the flat of her hand and swung it at my head. One of my tricks, for heaven's sake!

My right ear exploded, the carpet-level surrounds were suddenly brilliantly lit, dancing strangely, and there was a warm trickle down my face. I hung on for dear life.

And that was about it. If Karpov or any of his friends arrived, my parting remark to Potter about him being 'needed' in the case of my disappearance wouldn't be so hilarious.

She swung again, half missing, and her equilibrium suffered; the gun just clipped my head in another shower of stars. I was still pulling blindly at the ankles. She fell onto the bed, bounced off and slid down abruptly to my level. There was a sharp gasp and she was wincing; I guessed that she had scraped her backbone on an edge of the bed frame.

The damaged Fraulein continued to fight with – godammit! – skill, as well as fury. A stranglehold here, a wrist-lock there – plus sheer female tiger-like innovations. Good grief, was I getting some rough treatment tonight!

She tried to knee me twice mid the second time there was glorious vision of a tiny white, frilly triangle of something where I had no business to be looking, in the circumstances. In passing, I didn't think that that small item had been bought in the Moscow GUM Department store.

Eventually we both ran out of steam and there we were, subsided between the beds with telephone dangling on its cord and getting in the way of both of us. An impasse; but I was nevertheless in a superior position in what is known technically as a 'smother grip'.

We lay there, panting and heaving, each reflecting on the idiocy of the situation. Being at the 'upper' level, I was probably marginally more comfortable than her – despite what was surely a pulpy mess in place of one knee, the sole purpose of which seemed to be to signal dull, sickening waves of pain. A continuous quiet flow from the side of my face was dripping down and a great soggy red stain was clawing away at the thin cotton of spirited Christel's dress. I felt faint and desperately weak.

This girl could do one more thing to me. She could bite me. It sounds unusual, but it's been done before to good effect. Before she recovered enough to think about that, I hissed into her ear with as much authority as I could muster:

'It's no good calling, him ... brother Alex is at this moment being interviewed at Thai Police Headquarters…'

The body under me suddenly stiffened and I thought for one horrifying moment that the bell had gone for another bloody round. Then it all went limp, soft even, and I breathed long and deep.

Without disturbing my careful pinion arrangements at the top half of the ensemble, very slowly I swung my right leg round in front, keeping it stiffly straight. It wouldn't do anything else. I was now sitting up, more or less, on the slightly heaving belly of the occupant of room 301, which situation, in another context, would have driven the best of us silly,

If she had even sneezed in the direction of my right knee, I would have passed out then and there. Instead she looked at me with a face lined enough to be interesting and streaked with sweat, not tears:

'I smell clumsy British Intelligence…' she hissed between her teeth.

'I smell Lanvin's "Jolie Madame" – which is pretty fancy stuff for a KGB operative, isn't it?'

There was a short silence while we breathed fire at one another. Then the girl closed her eyes; some very white teeth pressed over her bottom lip and she moved her whole body just a little, screwing up her eyes. But it was *me* for heaven's sake – with the mangled leg.

'Okay. We have a truce,' I said. 'Just a few questions… In any case, you have no choice.'

Her pale blue eyes studied me for some seconds and then she nodded. The small-calibre pistol, I remarked, had been flung under one bed far out of anybody's reach. Not that it was of much use, except as a psychological deterrent.

I looked down again. The girl's Thai cotton dress around the shoulder and below was darkly blotched with my own blood. Very dramatic. The dress had been largely torn open during our wrestling and there was no question – it was a wild, wild scene.

I dragged myself up into a sitting position on the side of one bed. My adversary did likewise on the other. We sat there breathing quickly and viewing one another, like a pair of tired cats.

'Why, all of a sudden, is Moscow so interested in Henry Dobell?'

Chapter 12

'IT IS VERY OBVIOUS, isn't it?' Christel Scholze looked at me steadily, trying to guess how much I already knew. 'I will get some wet towels,' she added, to give a little more time to think. She pushed herself off the bed.

'Sit down!' I snapped. 'We'll clean up, later!' First things first. She lowered herself rather carefully, filled her cheeks with air and let it out through a pursed mouth with affected '*ennui*'.

'It is not "obvious" at all,' I said deliberately, 'There is no proper reason why the Russians should be interested in what Dobell was doing in Bangkok – it was just routine work...' Dobell's cultivation of a potential Chinese defector was another matter; but I wanted blonde Christel to volunteer information about that.

She shrugged her shoulders. 'I don't know. My job was just...' She stopped.

'Yes?'

'I don't know.'

I was becoming irritated. After all, I was supposed to have won a fine battle down there on the carpet.

'Listen. You have a nice comfortable air-conditioned hotel room here... Within an hour I can have you cooped up in a hot, stinking little cell down at Lartyau where the Thai Special Branch have time on their hands.'

She studied me coolly, not particularly impressed, but something must have occurred to her: 'I'm just part of the surveillance team and I also ran the listening post.'

'You must have learned *something!*'

'I knew who Wiley – or Dobell – was, but that's

about all. I didn't know who his visitors were—'

'But you heard the conversation...' I said.

'No. You can't monitor the voice on the machine – only the signal strength. I just gave the tapes to Alex... Karpov.'

'Where's the mike?'

She jerked her head in the direction of the cupboard. 'The ashtray...' She looked tolerantly at me in the belief that I had already found it. 'It needs replacing,' she added with a wry smile. 'The last two nights here, it was readable but the signal was weak.'

'Last *two* nights?' I said sharply. As far as anybody knew, Dobell had used the room for the day of the 14th only.

'Yes. The first session on the 14th, I think, was during the afternoon but the second, on the following day, went on quite late at night.'

'What did you get from the surveillance?'

'Not much,' she said ruefully. 'He usually lost us. But at the end we found something...' She paused and took a deep breath.

'Go on – you're still in big trouble!'

A floating expression of bitterness on her face gave way to studied calm. There was a certain weariness in her voice, too, which I didn't think was wholly explained by the recent physical exertions.

'He was careless and we followed him to a small house beyond the Pectburi district. We took photographs of the other man... It turned out to be the Chinese Chargé d'affaires. That wasn't exactly "routine", was it? Alex was very excited about it—'

'I bet he was.'

It was right. Dobell had recorded this meeting in a

northern Bangkok suburb; I had seen it on file.

'That's all?'

'Yes, except of course for the next night when he was kidnapped.'

'Tell me about that,' I heaved my swollen leg onto the bed. The sharp, shooting pains had died away in favour of a throbbing ache. 'And then we can think about wet towels.'

Christel Scholze'a manner seemed to change visibly. It was as if she had come to a decision that cooperation night lead somewhere useful. I doubted that it was the threat of arrest alone that had influenced her; she appeared to be too tough a character for that. She even offered me a cigarette, which I accepted gratefully.

'Well, we were watching him in town late in the evening – he was obviously up to something. But he made some more mistakes and we had no trouble in following him north of the city for some miles. There were only two of us in separate cars – Alex wasn't with us. With practically no traffic, we had to hang back a long way, changing places frequently and using different headlight combinations. We were all going rather slowly and a closed van overtook us. A little later something happened ahead – I couldn't see at first – but then I saw Dobell's car being forced to the side by the van. I stopped and turned off the light; our second car did the same – we had a sidelight signal system—'

'Why didn't you drive up to see what was happening, for crissake, it's unbelievable—'

'What would *you* do if you were following a Russian in an unfriendly country and it happened to him!' Christel Scholze's eyes flashed dangerously. I had said something out of place. I waved my hand to dismiss the subject. But spirited Christel was encouraged by my retreat.

'In any case, which side do you think I should have helped?' she said sweetly. She was needling me again, this cool blonde.

'Are you trying to pick a fight?' I said. Before she accepted I added quickly: 'What next?'

'From that distance, it wasn't very clear but I did see Dobell dragged from his car by a Chinese and he was then bundled into the back of the van. I don't know how many they were but there were shouts... It was all over so quickly. The van turned round, driving fast past me. I noted the number. Victor behind—'

'Victor?'

'In the follow-up car. He noted the number, too, and he's almost certain that it was the Chinese, Tan, driving the van.'

I had almost had enough. Never had I heard such a story. Peking Chinese just don't do this sort of thing. And yet there was Potter as well with his remarkable tale from Paris about the newly transferred Counsellor Tan soliciting an interview with me (of all people) to talk about Dobell's disappearance. If the Chinese were not involved, how did they even *know* that Dobell had missed out on last weekend's diving off Pattaya Beach. Oh, and a hundred other questions. Just one for the moment, however:

'Why is Dobell booked here until the end of the month – he had no need of the room?' Even as I said it, a vague and unlikely idea was flitting around in the back of my mind. Christel Scholze looked at me in what appeared to be genuine surprise.

'A friend downstairs told me he was going to stay on for a week or two...' I wondered which of the reception staff he had tied up. '… Then Alex later the same day – I think it was the tapes – said that Dobell was expecting an important contact soon. Dobell was then kidnapped, but Alex told me to stay on...'

She smiled at me with a mixture of amusement and contempt. 'Perhaps *you* are the "important contact"...'

In a sudden and rare moment of total loss of control, I swore at this cool, strong blonde who had done me so much damage. It was a vulgar, obscene even, expression delivered with vehemence. It was very un-British. I didn't apologise.

Christel Scholze looked startled for an instant but that was about all. Then I remembered that in theory I was master of the situation. 'Hot towels,' I muttered.

She went to the bathroom to see about it. I staggered upright and found that I could just about stand. My left leg would not bend without intolerable pain but it took a reasonable share of my weight. I hobbled to the dressing-table mirror to look at my face. Only half of it was visible.

I nearly fainted. I slumped forward, head buried in the crook of an arm. I didn't think of anything to say; it just came out in a pathetic moan: 'Dear God, what have I done, what *have* I done?'

'It's not serious. It looks worse than it is!' called a cheerful voice from the bathroom. Then she was there, sponging away, wringing out and sponging again; not quite tenderly but with a touch sometimes to be found in hospitals, if you're lucky.

'There – it's not bad at all!' said Christel finally. I ventured another look and brightened considerably. There were some lacerations below my right temple and a gash across the ear, the lobe of which had puffed up. But it was recognisably Lawson of old and I felt almost grateful to nurse Scholze.

'Move back to the bed, please.' If there's something I can't resist it is medical instructions. I limped across and propped myself up against the edge of one of the beds.

'You had better take your trousers off...' She was squeezing out yet another towel over a bowl on the dressing-table. I stared at her in confusion. She glanced back evenly. Full of bourgeois inhibitions, I bent down to roll up the relevant trouser leg from the bottom. But the knee had swollen to such a size that I could not ease the material above the top of the shin. I looked up with a crooked smile, but Christel had gone to the bathroom again.

My trousers were neatly folded on the bed by the time she came back.

It didn't belong to me at all. It was some prizewinning entry in a horticultural show. Even cool Christel grimaced at the sight of this bloated, multicoloured vegetable in place of my normal, elegant knee.

'There's nothing I can do for that. You will just have to wait until it goes down... You ought to have an X-ray.'

'Thanks – I'll—'

Somebody was knocking at the door. Instinctively I grabbed my trousers, without being able to do much with them in a hurry. If this was Comrade Karpov I was going to look very silly indeed.

'Who is it?' called out Christel, while I was trying to remember under which bed I had last seen her pistol.

'Laundry, ma'm...'

'Leave it outside – I'll collect it later, please.'

'Yes, ma'm.'

She was a very clean girl, Fraulein Christel Scholze.

'If you've cracked my patella, it will cost you dear,' I said. She didn't answer and left me again. Perhaps she had not understood the word 'patella'.

I found a clean shirt in my bag, mopped up a bit here and there on my suit and generally felt a lot better. I lit another cigarette and because there seemed to be a long silence from the bathroom, I moved over to investigate. The door was half open but I knocked discreetly.

'*Ja?*' She was standing there with her dress around her ankles, fiddling awkwardly with sodden bits of Kleenex trying to wipe away a long mess down her spine.

'For God's sake why didn't you say something?' I threw the cigarette into the WC, pulled out the plug of the washbasin full of discoloured water and snatched a clean hand-towel from a chrome rail. She didn't move except to fold her arms modestly. I dabbed and wiped with rare precision and, and ...

'It's superficial. It will dry up in a day or two, but you may be scarred for a time, I think.'

'Yes ...' She was looking at me in the mirror with a wooden expression of cool appraisal, which she managed so well. With everything else before me – back and front of this supple brown figure – I had trouble keeping my eyes on her face.

'I take it you're from East Germany,' I said. She stepped out of the dress in a pile on the floor and brushed past me to clatter hangers in the already brutally opened clothes cupboard.

After a decent interval, I tottered after her. She was shaking herself down into another light, cheap but fetching product of the local garment industry.

'Some of my family is in Leipzig...' she said, pushing

her blonde hair around with two hands. I didn't need to ask any more.

'Where are you staying – or is it an official secret?' she said with only a trace of sarcasm. As I didn't answer immediately, she turned and smiled. I thought it was a nice smile. Then she went back to sorting out her hair.

'I don't know,' I said, somewhat to my surprise. It was true – Potter had so far neglected to inform me.

Christel Scholze came towards me, shaking her hair back with a toss of the head. I could have been standing next to a magazine cover were it not for a certain disturbing warmth, a trace of Lanvin's confection in the air again and the fact that the face looked wiser and somehow more interesting than those generally seen on fashion plates.

Half casually, hesitant, she said: 'You can stay here, if you wish...' Again I was slow to reply, not through indecision but I was pondering on her motives. She touched my arm lightly and I thought for the first time there was genuine humour in her pale blue eyes: 'I don't kick in bed...' she said. I must confess I had even wondered about that.

'Thanks – but I'm sure arrangements have been made for me.' I picked up my bag, ready to leave. Christel didn't move.

'I need help,' she said, staring, down at the floor. Her voice had changed. There was a note of urgency in it rather than obvious despair.

'I know you do.'

'What – what are you going to do about me?' She glanced up, face set and trying not to betray fear.

'My advice to you is to forget tonight's little incident. But you might as well tell Brother Alex that there's no point in you, or anybody else, hanging round this hotel…'

'But he's... I thought you said he was...' She broke off and stared at me. Her nice suntan suddenly lost a shade or two, revealing a face torn between shock and cold fury. I opened the door quickly.

'*Du Scheisskerl!*' blonde Chrisel hissed at me. 'Yes… you *bastard!*' she added, in case I had not understood the first bit.

I rushed out before she could get her clogs on again. It would have been a fine exit if I had not tripped over the package of laundry just outside the door. But it wasn't a bad moment for all that.

Chapter 13

Paris

POTTER HAD NOT believed me but the round-up cable he sent to Head Office before we left Bangkok gave no hint of his inner thoughts. It was a modest account, stating that our enquiries had possibly identified one Christel Scholze as a member of the Russian surveillance team watching Dobell. The name was certainly an alias but Potter sent passport details and gave a physical description based on my alleged observations in the hotel lobby, just in case she had already come to notice elsewhere.

I had not owned up to breaking and entering, still less to any personal contact with that blonde athlete. My injuries, I claimed, were due to a swinging door and a fall in the Gents. I refused to discuss the matter further saying that 'it was so silly' and that I was 'embarrassed'. In fact, the face lacerations didn't look bad and the worst anyway was covered by a plaster patch. And Potter couldn't see the damage to my knee. He pushed his glasses up and down his nose a few times but he had no comment when listening to my short communication on the subject.

Why was I being so coy? Why not tell MI6 that Christel Scholze was not just 'possibly identified' as being involved but that she was up to her neck in the Dobell affair? Because, I suppose, in the first place, the information merely confirmed what they already accepted: that Dobell was being watched by the Russians at the time of his abduction. Second, there was something very odd about Dobell using the hotel on the second night for no recorded purpose and it was even odder that he had extended his booking there for a further few weeks without mentioning it to anybody,

If there had been some 'private' reason for the extra use of the hotel, it could scarcely have been connected with the kidnapping and I was reluctant to air information that might well ruin Dobell's career. I had been guilty of too many lapses myself in the past. Some other curiosities in Dobell's recent behaviour added to my hesitation, and I wanted to see what the Chinese had to say in Paris before drawing any conclusions.

So I kept quiet. And Ian Potter contained himself commendably. On the last leg of the flight back to Paris, as we took off from Frankfurt, I was leading two-one in a series of chess games we had played since leaving Bangkok. We would be in Paris in an hour, so Potter conceded and since we were travelling Economy Class (Houghton had stuck very firmly on that) he graciously paid for all the liquor consumed during the flight.

'You know, Dobell taught me to play chess a long time ago when we were on a course together,' I said, 'Well, I knew the rules before, but he really taught me a little about the game... He used to say that the key – and it's so easy to forget in the middle of a game – is to spend twice as much time thinking about the other fellow's possible moves than in plotting your own.'

'Would you give me the change in sterling, please,' Potter said to the stewardess. Then turning to me, he fingered his glasses 'I didn't realise you knew Dobell.'

'Well, like that – a little...'

'Hmm...' said Potter. He was thinking about something and it was probably not the Philidor's Mate that he had botched up in the last game.

We were back in the Embassy by the middle of the afternoon. Both the office and the surrounding high-class shopping area in the *rue du faubourg St Honoré* held some memories for me, not the least of which was the suicide of a tired old man who had been a collaborator of ours, just a hundred yards down the street. But that was two years ago.

Everybody fell all over Potter as soon as he showed his face – the *patron*'s return from faraway places. I was sadly neglected in a corner chair, suffering quietly with a stiff leg. It was still acutely painful to bend, but after many hours of light probing and other experiments, I had decided that nothing was actually broken.

Potter swept his fans away, signalled to me to wait and stalked into an inner office. Without being asked, a not quite friendly lady in her forties brought me *Le Monde* to read and a cup of tea. Potter was back in two minutes.

'Tan will see me immediately,' he announced. 'We're going to talk about Franco-China trade trends … You stay here. I'll be back in half an hour or so.' Potter was really getting on with it.

'I'd like to telephone,' I said. Potter paused as he went through the door.

'Use the one in the secretaries' office,' he replied and continued on his way. That wouldn't do at all, so I turned mournfully to study the rather special prose of *Le Monde*, which daily has perhaps the widest foreign news coverage of any newspaper in the world. Particularly on Asian affairs the political bias may be intrusive, but you can't have everything.

I had finished a second cup of tea and reached the paper's column entitled '*Agitation*' (social disorders, strikes, demonstration etc.) when Potter returned.

'Here it is then!' He handed me a slip of paper and drew up a chair. Printed with a biro-pen as before was Counsellor Tan's second astonishing communication to Potter.

'MR. LAWSON SHOULD COME ALONE TO LE REFUGE, 41 RUE LAFITTE, ILE DE LA DÉVIATION, CARRIÈRES-SUR-POISSY AT 9 PM TONIGHT'.

Simple, precise and no nonsense.

'*Tonight*?' I exclaimed. What was wrong with everybody? There was Potter off the mark again as soon as we touched home-base and Counsellor Tan seemed to be in a similar frame of mind. It was apparently only me who wanted a few hours' peace quiet to take stock of things – and to make a telephone call. After all, it was already two weeks since Dobell's disappearance; what difference would a few hours or even days make?

'That's what it says,' agreed Potter. I stared at the message again.

'Where in heaven's name is this "Carrières-sur-Poissy"? What is it – the Ambassador's summer residence?'

'It can't be far,' said Potter reasonably. 'They're checking next door...' He nodded towards the main office.

'Why couldn't I go to the Chinese Embassy just like you – scores of people go into that place every day without having their thumb prints taken?' I felt short of sleep and irritable..

'You are supposed to be the expert on Chinese

mentality,' said Potter coolly.

'There's *nothing* Chinese about this whole case as far as I'm concerned – that's the trouble!' I yelled. Potter was murmuring, 'All right, all right...' in a pacifying way when the efficient lady who had earlier brought me tea arrived with a map.

'It's to the north-west of Paris, a little beyond St-Germain-en-Laye,' she said briskly. 'No more than an hour's drive.' She was pointing to a circled spot on the map with a felt-tipped pencil. Potter adjusted his glasses with a word of thanks and the head girl left us.

'And what's this "*Ile de la Déviation*" – what kind of place-name is that for a good Chinese communist to choose for a subtle rendezvous?' I was half entertained by the thought, nevertheless.

'It is, according to the map, a small island in the middle of the Seine, which you get to by a bridge,' Potter said patiently.

'*Le Refuge...*' I found myself complaining '... That's a private house? A bar? A sanitorium?' It must have sounded very uncooperative. Potter looked at me sharply.

'Look,' he said not unkindly. 'If you don't feel up to it tonight, I'll try to contact Tan again and postpone it until tomorrow...'

I suddenly felt, with real embarrassment, that I was being unnecessarily obstructive. This was after all, why I was being paid, why I had been brought all the way from Mexico – to meet a Chinese at his request who was going to tell us about the kidnapping of Henry Dobell.

'I'll go,' I said shortly. Potter stood up quickly and loped towards the main office door.

'I want a side-arm,' I said.

Potter stopped in his tracks and turned. 'Out of the

question, I'm afraid…'

'I want a pistol,' I repeated. Perhaps 'side-arm' had been too formal. Potter remained in the doorway, very large, looking at me severely.

'The Director said that at no time were you to be given a weapon—'

'You can telephone Houghton immediately and tell him that I am not going to creep around the French countryside, in these circumstances, tonight, tomorrow night or any other night, without one…' Mildly delivered, but none the less persuasive, I hoped.

Potter was still for an instant and then took an exceptionally long breath which seemed to indicate exasperation.

'Well, I must admit that you seem to be accident-prone recently' he said with surprising softness. He turned on his heel and walked out. He was no fool, Potter.

He was back in less than thirty seconds and threw a small black leather bag into my lap. He had not had time to telephone anybody.

I examined the contents and smiled appreciatively. It was a neat .30 automatic of Belgian origins with a full magazine clip. Quite a few of these weapons are lying around the headquarters in London, not because more than a handful of operatives know how to make them work properly, but because somebody with an artistic bent on the staff years ago had written a treatise extolling the virtues of this gun with so much technical conviction that two gross were ordered immediately. The author of this treatise subsequently died of DTs and legend has it that in a last confidence he revealed that his enthusiasm for the Belgian firearm was entirely based on what he described as 'the sexually orientated butt'. This particular pistol, however, entered irrevocably into the folklore and administration of WRU. Not so at MI6, where they have other arms including the more military and weighty Browning 9 mm.

Still smiling gratefully and fondling the thing, I said:

'This isn't standard issue – how—'

'The Director had it sent over – in the event that you insisted…'

'Ah-ha,' I said gleefully and my smile stretched wider. For some seconds I was basking in the knowledge that Director Houghton had been obliged to take account of the attitudes of WRU in general and of the disgraced Lawson in particular.

'Ken…'

The moment dissolved. Potter had never before been so familiar; until now it had always been 'you' or some crass circumlocution. I looked up in some surprise.

'Yes?'

Potter sat down heavily, whipped off his glasses and started polishing them furiously with the end of his tie.

'My considered opinion is that you should leave it here.'

'Balls!' I said.

Chapter 14

Ile de la Déviation

EARLY THAT EVENING we drove out of Paris on the spiralling highway around the tall buildings of the office and residential complex called 'La Défense'. Thirty minutes after leaving this north-western edge of the city, we passed St-Germain-en-Laye and then took a wrong turning.

Encountering more of the local forest than seemed normal, the error became clear. Potter wrenched the car off the road onto a verge rather impetuously although we had plenty of time in hand. This manoeuvre earned us a lot of flashing lights and horn-pushing from following motorists one of whom, particularly irate, pulled in twenty or thirty yards ahead. He got out and tripped towards us, gesticulating in a threatening manner.

'Look at that clown,' said Potter quietly.

'Well, he did have to brake a bit...' I said, with the noise of screeching tires behind still fresh in the memory. Potter sighed and heaved himself out of the seat. As he stood up by the side of our Peugeot, his huge form was silhouetted by the headlights of following cars. Upset though he had evidently been, the Frenchman's advance faltered at the sight. Then he stopped altogether for an instant and finally turned to run back to his own car. Potter leaned on the door of the Peugeot blinking behind his spectacles, which sparkled against the oncoming traffic. I was laughing for the first time in six days.

'I don't think it was us after all,' he said. I was getting to like Potter more and more.

The map told us that we could continue for another mile or two and then double back along the bank of the Seine towards the *Ile de la Déviation*.

Soon we were delving through quiet cobbled streets sparsely lit in the thin night mist; old buildings hung over us on either side. Then suddenly we were by the river, cluttered at the edges by rows upon rows of the long barges of the Seine, some dark and gaunt, others with twinkling lights and a curl of domestic smoke above the wheelhouse quarters.

'Good heavens!' I said, holding a lighter to the map, 'This must be Conflans St Honorine... we ought to have a look around. It's a pretty place—'

'We turn off here.' Potter wasn't listening to me as he peered around, trying to read elusive signposts.

'I want to see the church and the ramparts,' I said.

There was no reply. Potter was still preoccupied with signs that seemed to be telling us to go back to St.Germain or even to Paris. 'It's a long time since I've been here,' I continued. 'One of the nicest spots near the city—'

'What the devil are you talking about!' Potter suddenly looked across at me, 'This isn't a tourist jaunt – it's business!' He swung a wrist around to look at his watch. 'Ten past eight – and we've got another fifteen minutes' drive!'

That still left half an hour, provided that we found the road, but Potter was dynamic once the whistle had blown.

'Let me have my fun – it may be the last I'll ever have...'

There must have been an excessively sober note in my voice. The Peugeot braked violently to a halt. It was an anxious moment. I looked behind again, but fortunately there were no immediately following cars. Potter revved up Brands Hatch style and yanked around impatiently with the gear lever. But he chose his words carefully

'Don't be so bloody melodramatic,' he said with slow emphasis. 'You're just going to a meeting with a Chinese, but rather carefully arranged – that's all!'

'The Chinese have apparently abducted our Henry,' I snapped. 'It could be a new element of their foreign policy to snatch British officials who go to carefully arranged meetings!'

Potter snorted and thumped his hand decisively on the steering wheel.

'Anyway, I'm in charge,' I said.

Potter jumped and turned to face me squarely in his seat.

'… Or I don't go to this meeting at all,' I added quickly. The engine was idling smoothly now; the car had been well looked after by the Embassy mechanics.

'Any of these streets to the left will do. They all lead up, and that's where the ramparts are… Besides, up there you can see the river – then we'll know which road to take.'

We moved off again with Potter still highly motivated by the idea of getting to the *Ile de la Déviation* on time.

'This one looks right.'

'It's "*Sens unique*".'

'Never mind – there's nobody around!'

A delirious thirty-second ascent up a winding alley with nothing coming down (otherwise all this would be in the third person and recounted with far less affection) and there we were in the *Parc du Prieuré*, Potter having parked unnecessarily on the crisp lawn behind the thirteenth-century *Eglise St. Maclou.*

A man was relieving himself against a hundred-year-old tree in a corner; he glanced nervously over his shoulder at me and then at the irregularly placed Peugeot. He zipped up very quickly and slid off into the shadows.

Potter remained in the car and I limped across to a parapet on the edge of the *Parc.* This terrace-like ledge overlooked the Seine winding away into the distance in a broad, pale strip. Apart from occasional yellowish street lamps in the section of the town below us, a few other lights flickered in the heavily wooded surrounds on each bank of the river.

The night sky, as everywhere near a big city, was not quite dark. Only the brightest of stars showed themselves as thin, uncertain pinpricks of light through a veil of high cloud. A calm, agreeable evening and a quietly impressive view of the Seine; in other circumstances, even the word 'romantic' could have been right.

I lit a cigarette. It was anyway a moment for reflection. I looked into the distance. Downstream, just a kilometre or two away, on a dark slither of an island, a Chinese with news of a kidnapping would be waiting. It was an extraordinary location for anybody to choose for a meeting, let alone a Chinese diplomat. And this particular Chinese had been cultivated by Dobell as a possible defector. Others might have seized the point more easily, but any meaning to this 'coincidence' eluded me and my mind kept turning over aspects of the Russian-supplied evidence.

The way the cigarette was burning down betrayed my agitation. From somewhere in the streets below, the rasp of a motor-cycle cut into the silence for a few seconds.

And then it was quiet again. It was a peaceful little town.

What the Russians were up to in this affair I could guess at – perhaps wrongly – but at least there were possible explanations. But the *Chinese*... I didn't know what to expect on the *Ile de la Déviation*, nor how to prepare for it.

It wasn't really cold standing there in that quiet, rather beautiful spot, but a sudden shiver flitted through me. Then, the slightest of noises just behind me made me start. I dropped the cigarette and wheeled round.

Potter stood there no more than a pace away, pushing at his spectacles and taking in my favourite Turner-like scene.

'Nice view,' he said casually.

'My God, why do you have to go creeping about like that!' I breathed out loudly and screwed the cigarette into the gravel with my good leg. He moved like a cat, this huge man. 'Or, even, *how* do you creep about like that?'

'I think we should go,' Potter said.

After twenty minutes of bumping along a pitted and muddy track that followed the bank of the river, we reached a point opposite one end of the island in question. As we went on, the dark hump in the middle of the Seine became wider and the channel on our side increasingly narrow.

Then we reached a partially asphalted clearing. By the riverside were two hut structures associated with the working of sluice gates of a lock. A single inadequate light fixed to the top of one of the huts illuminated the scene. It was no doubt well-meant, but the chief effect was merely to deepen the shallows. Fifty yards further on, a high metal footbridge spanned across to the island; the bridge, too, was lit at both ends in an energy-saving way. It was all rather eerie – and I hadn't even got out of the car yet.

'That's the access,' said Potter with a trace of wonder in his voice and looking at the bridge. He then pointed to some lights on the water from a building on the island about two hundred yards past the bridge.

'That will be "*Le Refuge*". It's a café used by the river bargemen... But in addition to the locals, a few people make the excursion from Paris at weekends. It's something different – mainly in summer, of course.'

Potter's last remark only added to the tension that had been building up. 'Why have you been keeping that so secret until now?' I asked tersely.

Potter looked at me, a little surprised. 'Yes...' he mused, 'I'm sorry – I wasn't keeping it from you... They only found out just before we left. I had forgotten...' He sounded honest.

'There's no other car,' I complained. 'How did Tan get here?'

Potter shrugged. 'He may not have arrived yet. I don't know – you can ask him.'

'Perhaps he won't be able to find the place,' I remarked hopefully.

Potter smiled and was delving in a door pocket. He handed me a hefty flashlight fully a foot long.

'You had better take this,' he said. 'They say there's not much of a road over there - and with your leg you don't want to fall into a hole!'

Fall into a hole? Good grief, I hadn't thought about that! Just what kind of a mess was I getting into? I weighed the thing in my hand. 'A chap could drown holding onto this, you know...' I gave it back to him. 'I don't much like torches,' I added. 'They give away as much as they reveal.' The door was open and I swung my good leg out.

'Ken, I recommend that you take the torch and leave the pistol behind.'

I jerked my head back to study Potter. His face was bland.

'Goddamit, you *do* go on, don't you!' I snatched the offending object from him. 'I'll keep the gun *and* I'll take the torch!'

Just before closing the door, I leaned forward a little: 'Thank you... er... Ian.'

After a few steps, I turned when Potter rapped on the windscreen. He nodded encouragingly and was waving with those small movements of the fingers that you use to a hesitant toddler who has just ducked out of immediate parental control.

I shone the searchlight in his face for a second and then stumped off to cross the bridge.

Chapter 15

POTTER WAS RIGHT. Although the track on the island was straight, it was rough, muddy and full of potholes. The only lighting came from occasional houses buried away in the thick vegetation on either side.

I used the torch – confound it all! – most of the way; it enabled me to keep to a narrow grass verge on the edge of the treacherous track. As I passed a small gate stretched across a gap in the hedge, a dog snarled at me: an honest bark would have been less threatening. Altogether it was an unpleasant approach to what would doubtless be a momentous rendezvous.

Soon, through the trees, I could see the lights of the café. I came first to a clearing on the left of the track, which evidently served as a summer terrace by the water's edge. Even tonight one or two of the half a dozen or so of the crude wooden tables were adorned with candles burning in jam-pots. But there seemed to be no clients who were fresh-air fiends. I walked on to within a few yards of the café-bar itself and looked through the top window portion of the door at the company within.

A man in overalls behind the bar was drying glasses while shouting encouragement at a noisy group at a table shaking dice for '421' in the game of that name. A handful of tipplers at the bar were drowning the disappointments of life in a habitual way, and a bargeman, by the look of him, in a corner was tucking into a great pile of *'frites'*, with a bottle of Heinz ketchup to hand. It wasn't exactly the sort of gathering where you would expect to find a senior Chinese diplomat.

'*S'il vous plâit!*' The voice came from the terrace behind.

I turned to find someone walking towards me. He was a slim man dressed in a dark raincoat, aged anything between forty and fifty. He looked, in fact, like a younger, taller version of China's sometime Prime Minister, Chou En-lai. He came closer and looked at me carefully. 'Just a moment, please...' he said in English.,

The Chinese slipped by and tapped on the glass portion of the door and signalled almost familiarly to the barman. Then he returned to me and, in the manner of a courteous host, he gestured to the gloom of the terrace: 'I am sitting over there... If you are not too cold, it is a pleasant spot and we can talk...'

All right. That was what I was there for. I followed him, to the appointed corner. We shuffled around, facing one another, with half a candle blackening the sides of the jam-jar between us. At last I chose to sit, after some idiotic oriental hesitation, with my back to the river rather than to the dark bushes behind or to the unpredictable café *clientèle* in front. No sooner had I hobbled round to my seat than the blue-overalled barman came up and looked enquiringly at me with unfriendly eyes.

On the table was an empty coffee cup and a small glass of some kind of alcohol scarcely touched. 'What's that?' I asked. 'Williamine,' said Counsellor Tan.

'Same thing, please... And a coffee.'

The Frenchman left us. The Chinese, speaking excellent English with only a trace of an accent, asked whether I had found the place without too much difficulty and then remarked on the picturesque aspects of the local setting.

He could have been making polite small talk across

anybody's dinner table. It was exasperating. But I presumed that he was waiting for the barman to serve me before getting down to business.

I studied the man closely. He had rather fine, regular features; his origins were manifest enough but without any exaggerated characteristics of the Asian race. It was a serious- locking, intelligent face and handsome enough to play the lead in a Run Run Shaw production. His confidence and relaxed manner were unusual for a Chinese official, most of whom have a sterner, more defensive style.

By the time the waiter returned, I had virtually abandoned my reluctant half-belief, which had been growing stronger as the evidence piled up, that the Chinese just might have abducted Henry Dobell; Counsellor Tan seemed far too 'civilised' and well-mannered for anything like that. The idea had always been fantasy, of course. I was beginning to feel considerably more at ease.

'*C'est tout ce qu'il vous faut, Monsieur Tan?*'

That suddenly jerked re upright as I was slouching into a more comfortable frame of mind. What the devil were the staff of *Le Refuge* doing – knowing the name of this Chinese diplomat who had only been in Paris for little more than a week? Tan waved the man away and then leaned forward on the table a little.

Add earnest and confidential to the other aspects and there you have the exact picture of Counsellor Tan of the Chinese Peoples Embassy at ten past nine one cool night, installed on the deserted terrace of an obscure cafe on an island in the middle of the Seine, and rather a long way downstream from the bits of the river in Paris which everybody knows.

His interlocutor? K. Lawson, reluctant 'agent' for the affair, sometime student of Chinese politics, summarily extracted from exile and there for the intrigue, a useful ex-gratia payment and because it was his duty to find out what Peking knew about the kidnapping of Henry Dobell. Bizarre? Yes – and it was also a nasty moment as the other man unfurled his cold spike of news:

'Listen carefully, Mr Lawson, this will be our only meeting... What I have to say is final and is in no respect negotiable. Henry Dobell is our hostage. He will be released unharmed on one condition. If the condition is not met, you won't be seeing him again...' the Chinese glanced at his watch in an unnecessary gesture, '... The business will be over and done with before midnight tomorrow.'

Chapter 16

I SAT THERE, rigid, and gaping stupidly. Questions half formed in a turmoil of mental excitement but everything seemed stuck in my throat. My mouth was suddenly very dry and I gulped at the fiery '*poire*', wishing that I had ordered a long beer instead.

'Wh – what condition?' I croaked.

'You will bring here tomorrow night at the same time the total equivalent of £400,000 made up of roughly equal amounts of dollars and sterling, all in used notes. You will then be told what to do next.'

I stared at Tan, the lines of his pale, serious face deepened in the yellowish flickering of the table candle.

Then I wanted to laugh. The feeling of relief was such that I almost threw the empty liquor glass over my shoulder. Tan was obviously a genuine psychopathic case and the Russians – God knows how – had identified it and were using this unfortunate Chinese official for purposes of their own. Without even thinking further, it would be a Soviet scheme to foul up Sino-British relations.

Within five minutes I would have Potter make his French connection at the first telephone call and Tan would be picked up by the Gendarmerie on some pretext. Suitable apologies and embarrassment all round at the Chinese Embassy first thing tomorrow morning – I was hoping I might be there to witness the scene. And all that Russian plotting – what a thing for friend Boris back at WRU to get his teeth into.

'All right,' I said, 'I can't speak for the government, of course, but I know that Dobell's safety will be the first concern ...' I stood up to leave, pulling my face into a beaten expression of sullen agreement. 'Tomorrow nine o'clock sharp, then...' I added, wondering whether to shake hands or not.

There was something in Tan's eyes that delayed my departure. He looked at me with a part quizzical, part tolerant expression; holding out his hand – but not very generously stretched – he was offering me something.

'You are more of a fool than I have been led to believe, Mr Lawson,' he said quietly while I gazed in a trance at the British diplomatic passport. It passed for being Dobell's and I thrust it near the feeble candle-power, thumbing through to the appropriate page to check the authenticating deliberate printing mistake. The light was hopelessly inadequate.

'Don't bother,' said Counsellor Tan easily. 'It really is his passport... You can keep it – he does not need it at the moment.'

This upset me for a second and I was breathing quickly. But very soon 'explanations' were tumbling through my mind; obviously the Russians had somehow got hold of it; perhaps Dobell had died and—

'Before you leave, you should also hear what Mr Dobell has to say himself...' Counsellor Tan delved into a briefcase at his side and produced a small Sony cassette player.

I sat down again, still incredulous, but unable to give expression to my doubts.

Then, at the sound of Dobell's voice, strained and slower than I remembered, the internal fidgeting of my stomach told me I was prey to an awful uncertainty.

'I am unharmed and not being ill-treated...' Then there was silence except for the soft hissing of the tape.

'Is that all?' I asked and really by then – I admit it – frightened to death.

Tan raised a hand. 'Wait…' he said softly.

A few more seconds passed with the tape still running, then at the same voice level:

'These people are serious negotiators…'

A faint click on the tape indicated that recording had finished at that point and the Chinese stopped the machine.

For all the passing of the years, it was, as far as I was concerned, Henry Dobell's voice. Mindful of the Russian technical operation against Dobell in Bangkok and the recordings they must have made, it occurred to me of course that this was probably a clever 'montage'.

'What was the gap – an accidental Watergate erasure?'

Tan almost smiled. 'He said something unnecessary – that's all…'

I looked at him, my mind bouncing from one extreme to the other. He sensed the confusion and uncertainty despite the unimpressed attitude I was trying to convey.

'It doesn't matter now,' Tan continued. 'I can tell you that it was a reference to a move in a game of chess – or so he claimed.'

The fidgeting inside gave way to honest upheaval; not a word could I articulate in protest.

'In fact, we tried to persuade him to plead for action to ensure his release,' the Chinese added smoothly. 'He knows what the terms are, of course…' Tan pressed a stud on the player and the slim cassette jumped up. '… But he refused. He is either a brave man or he is stupid – or perhaps just very British!'

The Union Jack was suddenly fluttering before my

eyes and in addition to the disturbances lower down, a lump came up in my throat. Counsellor Tan had a touching personal comment: 'My own view is that it was a mixture of all three things... Here – you should keep the tape as well. Even if there was time, it would be wasted effort to analyse it technically – it is genuine.'

I got a grip of myself and just at that opportune moment the barman came bounding across. I asked for a beer and once again Tan refused further refreshment.

'Now look, Counsellor...' I said emphatically, 'China enjoys good relations with the United Kingdom. It is inconceivable that the Chinese government would indulge in a vile criminal act – the kidnapping of a British official. It's monstrous and it's just not credible!'

The waiter returned and the Chinese paid him off.

'*Bonsoir, Monsieur Tan – merci!*' He retreated with a happy smile. Without a doubt, there was deference on one side and at least some degree of acquaintance was evident from the exchanges between this unlikely pair. Again the surprise registered but was blunted by the overall shock of Tan's other revelations.

'I am not here to listen to your expressions of disbelief and outrage – I am here to deal!' said the Chinese sharply. 'Moreover it is a transaction in which you have no choice if you want Dobell back alive!'

I stared at the man, fighting with a sudden hot rush of fury within, made worse by a growing sense of helplessness.

Perhaps it had been some slight sound or movement of air in the still night, but I looked quickly over my shoulder. What I saw made me jump as I turned round fully, for the moment uncomprehending.

A few yards away at the river's edge a long black

shape was sliding silently at the pace of a spreading stain. Then a voice, fully thirty yards away, called out once and a man carrying a loop of rope as thick as a wrist leapt lightly from the barge onto a ledge of the terrace just opposite our table. It was unnerving, the silence of that dark massive movement. Absurd, but my heart, was pounding away again.

'They often tie up here. The bargemen use the café...' Counsellor Tan said in his social, diplomatic way.

'So everybody keeps telling me.' I turned back to face the Chinese.

'It is not strictly relevant to our discussion,' he continued, 'but... I did not say that I was acting in the name of the present Chinese government.'

I was wrong. I thought we were finally through with surprises for that evening. But here was just another little point to ponder on. I scarcely noticed somebody squelching by on the track and I certainly wasn't concerned with the inquisitive mongrel who stopped a few yards away, one front paw in the air, wrinkling his nose at the international element on the terrace.

'*Viens, viens ici!*' called a man's voice from the track. The dog loped away. What *was* this Chinese getting at!

'I represent a group of what you in the West would call "dissidents"... We have considerable support among the military but the real base is the academic establishment. We are united in being anti-Mao and anti-Moscow. In western terms we might be called 'democratic socialists'... A sort of "third force".'

'Rubbish!' I exclaimed. 'I don't believe you – nobody has ever *heard* of such a group in China!'

'That may be true, but in Peking they know very well

that it exists... A lot of the political "campaigns", purification movements and reshuffling of top military commanders reported in the western press are explained by discovery of some part of the resistance. But they can't win... We have support in key places. We will not even have to wait long...' Tan smiled in the patronising manner of a professor correcting a student who thinks he has got it right already. '... But to return to our business, we urgently need these funds to finance certain propaganda and other action among overseas Chinese—'

'I don't accept a word you're saying!'

'Mr Lawson, it is a matter of indifference to me *what* you "accept" – the essential and only point is that I am demanding £400,000 for the release of Henry Dobell! Otherwise...' It was precise and coldly menacing. If it was bluff, it was not the sort you could ignore.

'Why the devil didn't you just *ask* for the money – you seem to know who to go to – instead of kidnapping a British official!'

'We would not have got the money...' Counsellor Tan replied simply. I stared at him speechless in the knowledge that he was probably quite right. If he had gone to the Americans, it could have been different. But given the rather special association with Dobell in Bangkok, the latter had no doubt been seized an ideal 'target of opportunity'.

A man dressed in baggy denims and a beret banged the door of the café coming out, glanced in our direction and strode off down the track. A child's voice came from behind and I turned to watch a woman holding the hand of a five-year-old leading him along the deck of the barge towards some steps at the edge of the terrace. A man came out from the wheelhouse to follow them; he was dressed in a curiously formal way in a jacket and tie. Steak and chips for the family at *Le Refuge*.

'Your position will not be so bright, will it, if we immediately inform the Chinese Embassy here of this little episode...?' It seemed a good point to make. The candle had now burnt very low and was spluttering the light was dancing with a discotheque strobe-like effect on the features of this remarkable Chinese. He smiled again.

'Arrangements have been made to cover that possibility,' he said quietly. Perhaps I looked sceptical because his smile widened. 'Apart from the consequences for your Mr Dobell, do you know what would happen? The Ambassador would ask me to draft out a full report for the Ministry indicating our amazement that the British authorities should engage in such absurd provocation—'

'But you're *here!*' I snapped and thumped the table. This made the glasses tinkle and it was the *coup de grâce* for the struggling candle, which went out with a blue flicker and that interesting accompanying smell. 'And there are witnesses!' I added, throwing my hand in the direction of the bar. Counsellor Tan's face was now just a faint disc in the dark. It suddenly came closer to me.

'But I was invited, Mr Lawson...' he hissed at me in an exasperated, conspiratorial tone, '... by the British Secret Service – to receive an important communication...'

Wrestling in the blackness with my doubts and perhaps just to give more time for reflection, what must be a commonplace objection came readily to my lips: 'That kind of money can't be found by tomorrow night.'

'Governments can do anything, as you must know, Mr Lawson.'

I stood up. 'My opinion is that *this* government will

refuse to have anything to do with it. So don't be surprised tomorrow night if a squad of French police meet you here instead of me!'

'If there is anybody on the island with you tomorrow night, it will be a disaster for ... for everybody,' said Tan evenly and more or less ignoring my opinion. 'One more thing,' he added. 'Take this, please – you should put the money in it.'

I used Potter's small crowbar of a torch to look at what was being offered. It was a plastic carrier bag, the top of which could be sealed by a sliding clip; it was the kind of bonus item supplied by some shops to justify excessively priced garments. I folded it up and put it in my pocket. 'And even supposing they agreed to deal, it would only be done *after* Dobell is delivered – we have no guarantee he's still alive even!'

'We will arrange for Mr Dobell to speak to you tomorrow night before you hand over the money.'

That, I must say, impressed me a little. But I didn't think that it would happen. The Chinese also stood up.

'How did you get here?' I asked. I wasn't going to offer him a lift back, but I was curious.

'We have quite a lot of friends, I assure you... So you will be here alone tomorrow night at the same time,' Tan said briskly.

'Don't count on it,' I said and turned to walk towards the cafe.

*

A dozen or more people were scattered between the bar and tables. The air was thick with a tobacco haze and the place was filled with convivial noise.

'I want to telephone, please.'

'The barman, joking and talking animatedly with several clients at the counter, glanced at me with no expression at all and just pointed to a telephone at one end of the bar. '*Encore deux fines à l'eau, patron!*' somebody said. He wasn't just the barman, he was the owner. I dialled one or two meaningless numbers and recorded voices told me all sorts of things in the earpiece.

At the rear of the counter on one of the bottle shelves were two old photographs; they were off-duty, military snaps and under one I could just make out something about 'Dien Bien Phu', the fall of which decades earlier had signalled the end of the French presence in Vietnam. I dialled another imaginary number. While ostensibly waiting for someone to answer, I made a conversational approach to the *patron*, who had his back to me.

'Nice to find an Asian who appreciates a good *poire*,' I said. 'Have you known Monsieur Tan long?'

The back remained turned away. The *patron* had certainly heard me; a slight movement of the head betrayed him. I replaced the receiver and edged along the bar. 'There was no reply – do I owe you anything?' Of course I   didn't but I wanted the man to say something.

Without looking at me, he dismissed the question with a casual flick of the hand. He was in his fifties, a little fleshy but looked as if he had had a good strong physique not long ago.

Once more: 'It's a fine spot you have here…' Monsieur Tan did well to find it…'

The conversation and laughter died away as the *patron* turned and looked at me squarely. It was as if I had launched a saloon insult. A lot of other faces were also turned in my direction. All he said, very deliberately, was: '*Bonsoir, Monsieur…*'

I sighed, shrugged and walked towards the door. The *patron* addressed the group at the bar loudly enough for me to hear: 'That fight has been over for a long time but there are still some accounts to settle…'

I went down the stops from the cafe with the door banging behind me. What 'fight'? What was he going on about? How was he getting along so well with Counsellor Tan? Those and a lot of other questions came to mind as I walked along the edge of the building to reach the track.

Looking onto the terrace, I was surprised to see a dark form still huddled over the conference table. The tip of a cigarette glowed suddenly and then the Chinese called out 'Good night!' I didn't answer and headed back along the track towards the footbridge.

Counsellor Tan had not told me how he had arrival at this out-of-the-way haven for old soldiers, sailors and secret agents. For one reason and another, it seemed a good idea to find out.

After thirty yards, I stepped back into the bushes and waited.

When will I ever learn?

Chapter 17

I DIDN'T HAVE to wait long. After only a few minutes, Counsellor Tan walked across the terrace to the track. He stood looking for some moments and apparently satisfied that I was already well on the way to Paris with astounding news, he turned and made off in the opposite direction.

I had just started to move after him when another man suddenly came into view at the side of the café. He was wearing a short leather jacket which shone a little in the outside lighting of the building. He had not come from the bar itself; at least he had not used the main door that I was watching. He, too, glanced briefly in my direction and then set off in the wake of Counsellor Tan.

That he was following Tan became immediately obvious from the way he moved. I rejoiced in this development because following the follower (if the latter did his job properly) would presumably lead to the same result, with the advantage that there was somebody between the Chinese and myself.

The procession had gone a hundred yards or so and the path had become darker; the lights of the cabins and small houses set back from the alley wore some way behind us. Every so often, I thought I heard small sounds through the trees on the left; the river was there, glinting palely where the vegetation was less dense.

Once or twice, too, there might have been blurred shadowy movements at the water's edge; the locals walking their dogs, no doubt, on the river path. They seemed to be keeping pace with our lot, however, on the deceptive track.

After another minute's tentative progress, I was becoming jumpy and my nervousness was growing with every step. Having stumbled twice in the blackness, my injured leg hurt abominably and I knew that I couldn't go much further in these conditions. Moreover, the pace seemed to be quickening.

Then, by a dim light on a pole thirty yards ahead, the man in the leather jacket stopped and peered down towards the river. We had been going slightly uphill and the track was now some twenty feet above the river level. Looking down, I saw an immediate steep descent – a drop of fifteen feet – then the ground flattened out more gently to the bank. The light probably marked a path leading down, which I didn't think I could negotiate with the nimbleness of foot that the occasion demanded.

The brave attempt to glean some insight into Counsellor Tan's travel arrangements would have to be abandoned; instead I would consult with the man in front, in the hope that he knew something useful.

He was still there, crouched down among the shadows, but some feeble shaft of light played on part of that ill-chosen jacket. Very carefully I edged closer until he was only ten yards away. How should I address him? 'Psst...'? And if so, in what language – French, English, Russian? Or even Chinese?

A decision was deferred for a second because the man suddenly half-straightened and moved a step watching intently something down by the river. A slight hesitation and then he made as if to go down the steep path. Another second and he would have been gone forever.

I was carried away by a rash, instantaneous response, remembered no doubt from some thrilling cinema sequence: Potter's torch placed on the soggy turf of the verge, then neatly switched on and me, a second later, hobbling around in the centre of the path.

'*Arrête ou je te descends!*' I said, in what was hopefully a convincing growl.

The man froze, still half bent over and staring back, white-faced, at the torch. Then he heard me splashing towards him, from a different quarter, through the puddles on the track. He turned slowly and I was happy to see that his hands were already half raised without being asked. He could now see the Belgian comforter trained on him.

I ventured nearer for some confidential discussion. With the total preoccupation with the target, I found myself stumbling even more on this swampy public thoroughfare, which was such a disgrace to the Town Council of Carrières-sur-Poissy. And then a final, fateful step. Why, oh why could I not have been content to talk to this man from four yards away instead of three?

It was the rotten log which did for me. It went down suddenly in a deep pothole full of water. As the log touched bottom, the jarring pain seared up and brought me to my knees, falling forward.

The leather-jacketed one, evidently no slouch, sprang at me, hardly believing his luck. He made for his gun hand before I could do anything with it. We struggled in a heap in the mud. No question of standing up and decently socking one another from one side of the track to the other; no, it was just the dirtiest of alley fighting, with stiff fingers jabbing here and elbows and knees pummelling there.

He was strong, adept and – despite a deep elemental groan at one stage – he was winning. He was on top of me and half my face was pressed into the mud by an iron forearm across my throat. With his other hand he held my wrist outstretched, the gun still technically in my possession but unusable.

My head was gradually being pressed into the accommodating track. The desperate desire not to drown in four inches of muddy water provoked a frenzied effort and I managed to raise my face a little and gulp air. But you can't think of everything at once. That gesture had cost me concentration on my right hand and the fast-mover above wrenched the gun away,

He still had his arm across my throat and then I felt the cold snout on my forehead. In final despair I looked up at the man's face. It was a tortured face; small muscles were involuntarily twitching everywhere. His soft, terrible moaning was interrupted by gasps of breathing. The man was in agony

'You crushed them, *salaud d'flic!...*' He jabbed the gun violently into the space between my eyes. '... Yours is *now!*' he hissed.

There was a dull thud which filled my skull.

So this is what it's like to have your head blown off.

*

It was some seconds before the reality of still lying there, conscious, in the mud of the *Ile de la Déviation* struck me.

The gun had misfired. I think I understood this an instant before the other man. More last minute, inspired death-struggle heaving and I could hear metallic clicks as he pulled the trigger again and again, and all the while making strange whimpering sounds. Then a voice called out in French:

'For God's sake, what are you *doing!*'

Then an arc of light swept round, dancing on the tall hedging; it was no doubt Potter's torch. I was half sitting up still locked together with this man who felt so damaged that he was about to kill me for it. Then the light swung dizzily for an instant before a brighter flash coincided with a sudden razor-sharp pain at the back of my head.

I was stunned but not unconscious. I was aware of the other man disengaging himself and fragments of French dialogue.

'Look at him – the bastard cop!' The mud seemed to be growing warm under the weight of my face.

'Yes, but he's not French, *connard!*'

Somebody was ferretting in my pockets.

'Who cares – he got me and he knew what he was doing…'

'A bit of massage down the road will put it right... No, *leave* that!'

I think it was Dobell's passport they had found.

'This sodding gun is a toy – it doesn't work!'

'Just as well… Give it to me.' A short pause and a dog began barking a few hundred yards away.

'No, it's not a toy... there's something wrong with it.'

Another brief silence and then I heard a faint splash somewhere.

'What did you do that for?'

No answer.

'Come on – let's get back,.. *leave* him, I tell you!'

A heavy boot swung from a yard away had just landed in my back. I grunted instead of screaming. I thought there might be worse to come if I appeared unnecessarily aware of events. Yes, those things count when you're on the losing end.

I heard them go away. I could have slept or died comfortably then and there. But I dragged myself up, only to trip over Potter's blunderbuss of a torch which no longer worked in the way intended. I picked up the wretched thing and staggered back towards the bridge.

I now hurt all over, which at least enabled me to forget about my leg; the most distracting aspect was dizziness and a blinding hangover ache from the crack on the head.

Two late evening strollers passed by, staring curiously in the near blackness at the shambling figure and giving me a wide berth. Then I heard somebody gaining on me from behind. Surely, going in the same direction, there was a chance this person might offer a helping hand.

It was the man with the dog who I had seen earlier on the terrace. He also skirted by me on the opposite side of the track, peering furtively at the slower traffic. But the dog – some ill-defined but affectionate hybrid – came up, dallied a little, sniffed gingerly at my sodden trousers and was actually wagging its tail. Ah... a little sympathy at last! But not for long. '*Viens, viens ici!*' called a voice urgently twenty yards ahead,

After pulling myself up the steps of the high footbridge I had to rest. Slumped over the hand-rail in the middle of the span I looked down into the black depths below.

A thin sickle-moon had appeared and was faithfully reflected on the mirror surface of the water. I felt that a nice round, orange, full moon would have better suited the general lunacy of the evening. And I knew for sure that the version we had tonight couldn't be the twelfth crescent. 'Because the hero's crescent is the twelfth', according to the Irishman William Butler Yeats, who knew a thing or two about the moon. And heroes.

Further upstream I could see the dark sluice gates of the lock; the massive wooden blocks seemed to bulge like a wrestler's pectorals. But I welcomed the sight of that forbidding structure. It meant that my little expedition was nearly at an end.

Even the few minutes' pause had been a mistake. As I heaved myself upright and made my legs work again, everything had gone stiff, and dull aches came from bruised places I had not thought of before. I tottered off the bridge towards the clearing.

Whether it was because no more surprises were registering with me that evening or whether I half expected it, I'm not sure, but the car had gone and there was no sign of Potter.

I wandered around outside the huts for a   few minutes; I don't know what I was looking for and in any case I didn't find it. The blow on the head was no doubt affecting me because I even struggled round to the back of the premises to the dangerous water's edge to see if Potter had accidently reversed into the river. Then I opened a fencing door and there was a bedlam of squawks and scurrying from a crowd of hens belonging to the enterprising lockkeeper.

Lights were showing from occasional homes further up on the left, so I trudged off along that miserable obstacle course to look for an access path.

Suddenly, a car being driven furiously in low gear came sliding round a bend ahead; it came towards me, headlights everywhere, bouncing around on the pitted road as if it were being exercised on one of those demonstration runs for the manufacturer's guarantee.

I just stood there gazing stupidly into the blinding light, too weak and too tired to go anywhere if the vehicle happened to be aimed at me. It stopped miraculously a matter of yards away and the headlights dipped. The motor was still running. Then a very big man came bounding round and stood for a moment in front of the lights, staring at this tatty wreck.

'You're late again,' I said. I seemed to be swaying in the glare and I put a hand up to shade my eyes. Potter leapt forward.

'Good God, what *have* you been doing!' he said. Then he bundled me into the car with the first friendly touch of the evening.

I really just wanted to sleep or at least crumble into the passenger seat without having to speak. Potter was grinding the gears furiously, backing and turning to get the Peugeot faced the way it came. 'There's a main road half a kilometre ahead,' he said in an encouraging tone.

'Fine time to leave me,' I wailed.

'I heard a car start up further along this...' a bucketful of brown water suddenly splattered against the windscreen '...this bloody lane and I went after it. It was hopeless – they were too far ahead to see anything. Then I came back to get you.'

He swore again as the car lurched into another trough and he banged his head on the roof. I just moaned in general discomfort. 'What happened to you?' he added.

'Oh, I saw him... I'll tell you about that in a minute, but first you will want to know that I was beaten up.' I looked hard at Potter. He glanced back and pulled a face. 'That's what it looks like...' he said with apparent concern.

I dragged out his long torch from a pocket full of mud and handed it across to him. 'It got broken, I'm afraid.'

'Ah – here we are!' Potter said as we swung onto the blissful surface of a metalled road. 'Well, too bad,' he added about the torch, 'but I hope it was useful.'

'Oh yes – somebody bashed me on the head with it.'

Potter jerked round suddenly and while he was still looking I had a further word to say: 'The gun and a malfunction…'

Potter's eyes returned to the road and he pushed nervously at his spectacles, shining from the glare in front. It was a long time before he replied.

'I advised you not to take it, you know…' It was a soft, almost reproachful remark.

'Yes…' I said. 'Thanks…'

Then I dropped into a post-operation sleep – full of nightmares. Or recent memories.

Chapter 18

Paris

THE NEXT TWO or three hours passed in the blurred twilight zone of semi-consciousness and it was not unpleasant in retrospect. Potter took me home to his family den in the green, well-ordered and expensive Paris suburb of Neuilly-sur-Seine.

I remember walking past well-kept lawns to an apartment block and then being propelled into a brightly lit and silent lift, which took us up one or two floors.

Then there was Potter in a gleaming bathroom full of steam, running around with towels over his arm like a swimming-pool attendant, and me clutching on to some convenient chrome handle under a soothing warm shower. I recall, too, feeling ridiculous wrapped in one of Potter's vast bathrobes and being led gently to small bedroom with its own washbasin, unneeded in the circumstances.

'No,' I lied, 'of course I don't want to get into bed – let us sit a while and discuss matters seriously…' Did I really say that? Then giant Potter was feeding me giant whiskies while I recounted the extraordinary encounter with Counsellor Tan.

We came to no declared conclusion about those Frenchmen trailing the Chinese, Potter's casual opinion that they were 'common thugs' out to rob an evident foreigner, Tan, was scarcely convincing. Too tired to argue, but I was convinced that in view of the devotion of the French Communist Party to Moscow, the two at whose hands I had suffered could be local hirelings of the

KGB.

'They have a quarter of the French population to choose from,' I thought aloud. Potter didn't react at all.

I went to the bed and spent some time arranging myself in the most comfortable position on the well-sprung mattress. The last thing I heard just before the door closed softly was a half-whispering child's voice:

'Daddy, why was that man in such a mess?'

'What are you doing up – go back to bed ... *now!*'

'But why -?'

'*Ssh* ...!'

*

Some noise in the household woke me. My watch said it was 8.15. Turning over, with a twinge in every muscle, I closed my eyes again with a great sense of comfort that came as movement stopped. Moreover, I was blissfully relaxed in the knowledge that unless Potter became unreasonably bureaucratic, there was probably no need for me to stir for at least another week.

I didn't believe for a moment that the British government would entertain Counsellor Tan's proposals. In the first place, the idea of even 'dissident' Chinese being actively involved in the kidnapping was hardly credible. Secondly, I was quite sure that London would not accept that 'dissidents', in the coherent sense suggested by Tan, existed in China. Lastly – strictly irrelevant in view of the rest – I didn't believe that MI6 would fork out nearly half a million pounds to secure Dobell's release from anyway less than proven captivity; Dobell was virtually at the end of his career, and Head Office would make a business equation...

Much later, I woke and studied through half-closed eyes the doormat. Then I realised that it was not the doormat but a large brown suede boot. Potter had arrived carrying a breakfast tray. What a happy awakening – being brought breakfast in bed by MI6! I sat up and found that that the long rest had done wonders for my battered self. I also felt what might be called 'bright and cheerful' – meaning in this case, a state of mild intoxication at the sight of Potter blinking at me behind a pile of croissants and holding the *Sèvres* coffee jug poised in one hand: 'Black or white...?'

'I say!' I exclaimed with that special emphasis, which, in some circles, denotes joyful surprise.

'How are you feeling?'

'Fine, fine...The sleep put me right.'

'Well,' I take it easy... You'll find some newspapers in the salon. I'll be back later.' Potter left before I had a chance to ask him why he had not brought the newspapers in with the coffee. Perhaps it was expected that after all I would be dressing for lunch.

After breakfasting in a leisurely fashion, during which my main preoccupation was not to drop croissant crumbs in the sheets, I got up, washed and shaved and found a change of clothes from my suitcase, which Potter had thoughtfully left in the room.

Venturing out, it appeared that the apartment was empty. On the way through to the salon, however, I encountered a stout, strong-looking Portuguese maid: leaning on a broom in the hallway.

'*Bonjour, madame!*'

'*Bonjour, monsieur.*' She was looking at me sternly and I had the impression that Potter had left instructions that she should trip me up with the broom if I tried to leave.

It was almost one o'clock before my peaceful reading was interrupted. Potter's wife arrived, introduced herself and within ten minutes we were round the lunch table: *salade niçoise*, assorted *charcuterie*, chunks of *pain de campagne* and half a bottle of cheap red wine unfinished from the day before.

She was tall, striking woman from one of the hunting counties, who moved with an easy stately grace; her voice was low-pitched and she talked with a lot of charm and wit. We had an agreeable lunch spent in discreet conversation about beagles.

Potter himself arrived at 2.30 p.m. just as we were finishing the meal. He glanced at me and muttered 'Good!' to nobody in particular and then greeted his wife with proper affection, asking whether so-and-so had telephoned about the new sink unit. He then turned to me.

'And how do you feel now, Ken?' He was polishing his glasses vigorously with a large handkerchief.

'Perfectly all right,' I said. 'The rest was all I needed – I'm in good shape.' Given the rough treatment I had received, that reply made me a tough, resilient character. 'And your wife had just given me a marvellous lunch,' I added, smiling at Mrs Potter, who was clearing away the meal things with the help of the brute of a Portuguese maid. Potter's wife smiled back, dismissing the hospitality with a remark about mere 'leftovers'. Then Potter and I were alone.

'Well, we're going through with it…' he said in an offhand way.

Suddenly all the sense of relaxation in comfortable Neuilly evaporated.

'Of course, my leg is giving me a lot of pain and I

can't bend my back properly after the kick in the kidneys,' I said, unable to believe my ears.

'It was decided at the emergency CISA meeting early this morning. Charles Houghton, after explaining that he was obliged to regard the proposition as bordering on the lunatic, said that he preferred to leave the decision to the Foreign Office. The F.O. representative got approval directly from the Minister—'

'How do you know all this?'

'Scott-Baker, who was at the meeting, arrived here half an hour ago… He also brought with him the sterling component of the sum demanded by Tan.' Potter gestured to the carrier bag he was holding.

'Where do we get the dollars?'

'From the bank.'

*

Late in the afternoon, we drove to the elegant *Place Vendôme* where the needle column in the middle has had several different statues on top during its history; first it was Napoleon in Caesar's garb, who was soon replaced by Henri IV; the latter gave way to a *fleur-de-lys* before Louis-Philippe put Napoleon back, this time in military uniform. The column was torn down in 1871, only to be re-erected by the Third Republic with a replica of the original Napoleon statue at the top. It's anybody's guess who its next incumbent will be.

Potter left the Peugeot alongside some emphatic red curb markings. We walked through an archway in the seventeenth-century façade to reach the premises of a small private bank with a very English name. It was past normal business hours and the door was locked.

A slim, grey-haired man wearing pince-nez came to the door to let us in. He was exquisitely dressed in a conservatively cut three-piece, dark, pin-stripe suit and a silver-grey tie. A thin watch-chain was slung across his waistcoat. Exuding a firm, old-world manner, he seemed to be the ideal banker.

The handful of tactful staff still engaged in tidying up the day's business took no notice as Potter and I were led into the sombre but plush ante-room to the manager's office. Potter told me to wait and look after the 'sterling' packet while he went into the inner sanctum.

He returned in less than five minutes carrying the bulging plastic bag supplied by Counsellor Tan. We were then escorted courteously to the door.

As we walked through the passage leading to the wide footpath of the *Place*, Potter handed the bag to me. Of course I had never before seen the equivalent of £400,000 in bank notes, let alone carry it, and it was a lot heavier than I expected.

'Is this real money?' I said.

Potter ushered me carefully into the passenger seat of the Peugeot. 'Yes,' he said and shut me in.

Once we were on the move, I slid open the top of this well-filled package. It was a giddy moment: thick wads of notes of various denominations. A beautiful sight. But it didn't entirely explain to my satisfaction the weight of the bag. So I delved deeper.

Without dragging it out under the idle eyes of other drivers as we crawled along the well-lit, traffic-clogged rue de Rivoli, I quickly identified the hefty form of a Browning 9 mm at the bottom of the pile.

I sat staring ahead for some seconds without being particularly aware of two juveniles who were making faces at us through the rear window of the family saloon immediately ahead.

'It's mine,' Potter said. 'For God's sake be careful what you do with it…!'

Chapter 19

ANY MISGIVINGS which I may have had about continuing the job were obscured by the sheer speed of events. After leaving the bank, Potter drove us into an adjoining street, and manoeuvred the car into a space reserved for French Post Office (*PTT*) vehicles. He then went off to make some telephone calls.

I sat in the illegally parked Peugeot wondering whether I wouldn't do well to abscond then and there with almost half a million pounds in my lap. The car was likely very soon to be towed away by the Police anyway. Still, at least I would be able to pay the fine on the spot.

Potter had been gone five minutes when a stiff-faced *PTT* employee, who had just arrived in a three-wheeler yellow postal delivery van, rapped on the window and glared at me. I opened the window a fraction to let in some powerful advice to the effect that only a dolt of a peasant would park in a space clearly reserved for official vehicles.

In an apologetic tone I replied that it was 'for only two minutes' and that 'anyway, with your little tricycle, there's plenty of room in front'. But I was very anxious indeed, let me tell you. He was a youngish chap and no doubt the blue peaked cap with the thin white stripe had gone to his head. He became enraged and started to threaten me with official sanctions.

The abuse was still flowing on, so I wound down the window fully and pulled the Browning 9 mm from the plastic carrier bag. I pointed it at his nose. 'Go away,' I said.

It is, of course, an intimidating weapon, especially if

you are looking down the barrel at close quarters. I would never have thought, however, that outraged fury could dissolve so quickly into cringing panic. The Frenchman's face was suddenly transformed into a silent, twitching mask; he spread his hands in a half conciliatory, half pathetically irrelevant protective gesture. He backed away quickly, hardly daring to look over his shoulder on the way. At the curb he tripped and more or less fell into the arms of a passing honest citizen – one of many on the busy *trottoir*.

No doubt in the belief that he had found a friend, he pointed back to me in the car, evidently informing the bewildered pedestrian of his experience. The passer-by was a decent- looking fellow dressed in a short white jacket – perhaps an assistant from the local *pharmacie* nicking off for a five o'clock prescription at the corner café. He looked back at the Peugeot in frank disbelief.

I leaned out of the window with an understanding smile: 'It's the warmer weather...' I called out, winking theatrically. The chemist's assistant – if indeed he was such – smiled faintly and turned to be on his way.

The *PTT* official, aghast, was tugging at the clean white sleeve, pleading for another hearing. But the discerning chemist shook him off with a sharp word. The postman looked desperately after the retreating white jacket for an instant and moved a pace or two towards another pedestrian who stepped into the cutter to avoid him. After another appalled glance towards me, he darted forward to the   Post Office's main entrance.

There I saw him pushing furiously against the heavy glass-centred door. He seemed to go on pushing for rather a long time. I was genuinely becoming anxious by now; if Potter didn't return soon, there might be a real scene which we could scarcely afford at that stage.

Suddenly the pushing stopped and the door flew open more or less catapulting the lightweight Frenchman to the wall. The towering form of Potter stepped out quickly – he had evidently been pushing the door from the other side – and he turned to shout at the luckless *PTT* employee backed-up against the wall.

Potter stalked towards the car, muttering over his shoulder. He got in and slammed the door.

'Bloody Frenchman – shoving at customers like that! A postal worker as well!'

He ground the gears and we took off with some *élan*. At the end of the street I ventured a look behind. A mixed group of be-suited and overalled *PTT* personnel had been called to the scene. There was a lot of arm-throwing going on, observed by curious members of the public, but nobody, as far as I could tell, was shouting 'Stop thief!' in our direction. But we had got away with something and I sighed with relief.

'What's the matter with you?' Potter said irritably.

'Nothing,' I replied. 'I just don't like sitting around with £400,000 in a shopping bag. Tell me,' I said, to change the subject, 'was Henry Dobell ever in France?' It was just making casual conversation.

Potter was driving much more carefully now – too carefully for some behind us who tooted or flashed lights as we were relatively slow off the mark at traffic signals going up the Champs Elysées. Of course, in England, most people actually *wait* for the green light before accelerating.

'Oh, I think he had one routine here… but it was a long time ago – in the early Fifties.' Potter leaned forward a little and became very attentive to the road, We were at the Arc de Triomphe where the intersection of what used to be the Place de l'Etoile is now called Place du Général Charles de Gaulle. It is a mark of what he meant to the nation that the French understandably ignored the spirit of the General's last wish that his name should not be attached to public monuments.

Potter was manoeuvring in low gear, head rigidly turned to the right as we edged round the most hair-raising traffic pressure point in Paris. '*Priorité à droite*' is the rule but not everybody seems to believe it – least of all the insurance companies who in almost every case apportion the blame to both parties in the event of grinding metal and shattered glass at such places. He wound round unscathed and it was Potter's turn to sigh as if he had got away with something.

'Why do you ask?' he said.

'Oh, I don't know... I just wondered.' It was true. It had been an idle question without me really being aware of what prompted it.

We drove on towards St-Germain-en-Laye and Potter explained some of the wheeling and dealing that had gone on in London before agreement had been reached.

'If it wasn't literally a matter of life and death, the performance of the CISA would be laughable... Do you know that the funds were virtually released for the wrong reason!'

'What do you mean?'

'Well, Houghton refused flatly to use the Special Operations Fund – or any other - to pay the ransom. He argued that it was a matter of principle. Then, during the meeting there was a flash from Washington saying that the Americans had at least received fragmentary reports over the last year about an organised "dissident" group in

China; the information had never been published because none of the analysts believed it.'

We were still driving more slowly than the mass of traffic and a lot of impatient heads turned to glare at us as cars pulled out to overtake the Peugeot. I noted that Potter was frequently looking in the rear vision mirror. I wanted to ask about that but I was too fascinated by the London business. Potter was continuing:

'The others at the meeting seized on this and persuaded Houghton that the SOF would be properly used in financing Chinese dissidents - and more or less ignoring the ransom issue. He said it was "near lunatic", that he didn't accept that such a Chinese "third force" existed, but he finally agreed after getting the other members to note formally his reservations. Anyway Ralph Baker put him in a corner by pointing out that we had spent much more money in the past for even more dubious reasons—'

'Brave thing to say -'

'But the laugh, if it can be called that in the circumstances, is that the other committee members didn't believe the "Chinese dissidents" aspect either. Neither the Foreign Office nor the Security Service, for example, normally have the slightest interest or say in how the SOF is used – they just wanted, out of purely humanitarian motives, to get Houghton to pay the ransom.

'It seems to me,' I said, 'that Counsellor Tan has, through luck or insight, formulated his demands very well...'

Potter grunted his agreement and swung the car into an access road running parallel to the main highway. We were just beyond Rueil-Malmaison the on the N.13 and still in a built-up area. He stopped in front of a small café outside of which were a few canopied tables. It was 7.30 pm 'We eat here,' he said. It appeared to me to be a dingy sort of place but Potter had spoken decisively so presumably there was no choice.

We arranged ourselves at a table and I placed the bulging plastic bag between us on a spare metal chair with spindly legs. Would the next customer who sat there on the flaking yellow paint sense a certain thrill?

A DS Citroen pulled in and parked some twenty yards down the access road. Nobody got out.

Now Potter is alert as well as tall and he had certainly noticed this but he was giving orders, unconcerned, to a remarkably civil waiter. It is extraordinary how the attitude changes once outside Paris itself; no more of the often savage boorishness of a lot of those in the city who are supposed to pander to the public's needs.

Potter settled for a 'sandwich rillettes' with a pot of gherkins and a beer. I couldn't face real food – yes I was knotted up inside– and my modest request for a carafe of red wine and peanuts was greeted by derisive smiles from both Potter and the civil waiter. But everything was all right when I specified that I wanted the peanuts unwrapped and in a bowl; with an extra dose of salt. And the carafe of Bordeaux left on the table. Potter frowned at that.

'All right, what is that lot doing?'

'That's the backup vehicle,' said Potter in a somewhat exaggerated 'patient' tone. 'The Peugeot isn't exactly a Securicor van, you know…'

'Don't they want refreshments too?' I suggested.

'They stay in the car,' Potter growled. He was attacking the sliced *demi-baguette* with its rillettes stuffing as if he were playing the flute – with enthusiasm. It made me feel sick even to look at it as I toyed with my cheap red and peanuts. Potter, sensing my unease, said apologetically: 'I didn't have any lunch.' True, true – I had even polished off his wife's leftovers that day.

Yes, as an afterthought, I could imagine: 'they' in the DST* Citroen were probably armed to the teeth and it wouldn't do at all for them to be clanking around the peaceable surrounds of a pavement café on the outskirts of Rueil-Malmaison.

'By the way,' said Potter in between mouthfuls and reading my thoughts, 'I've alerted the DST... Without going into details, I told them that the meeting tonight involved the physical safety of one of our officers. Grillon wasn't very happy, but he agreed to have half a dozen people staked out round the place.'

I sipped at the last of a third Ricard. 'That was most unwise,' I said soberly. I wasn't quite sure why it was 'unwise', except that it meant yet another crowd of thugs in a position to leap out of the bushes at me on the sinister Ile de la Déviation.

'Oh, don't worry – they won't interfere. They will be there just to watch for anything unusual...'

'Unusual'? The word seemed to me something of an understatement. I looked anxiously at Potter, but he was paying the bill so I didn't complain further.

During the rest of the journey, we went through the whole thing again; all the absurd but indispensable minutiae associated with clandestine life: torch signals, flashing headlights, horn tooting and, in extremis, a few rhythmic rounds from the Browning 9 mm. I think I had

---

* DST – Direction de la Surveillance du Territoire (French Security Service).

got half of it right by the time we were bumping along the riverside track.

Then we were there, calmly, in front of the waterworks at 8.45 pm, exactly twenty-four hours after our earlier visit.

Quite deserted, no other cars, the same dim light high up on the sluice-gate shed, but in general an even darker scene than that of the previous night because the sky was overcast. Potter had switched everything off and we sat for some time in silence with the car windows wound down.

Quite apart from the immediate business, the terrain just looked moody and dangerous; nobody in his right mind would go wandering around such a place with a wallet in his pocket let alone our bundle of ready cash.

'Look, Ian,' I said. 'Why don't I stay here coordinating matters and *you* dash across to the island...' I paused as another thought struck me. 'Alternatively, why don't we *both* go? Nobody's going to filch your car – it's got diplomatic plates and, and...'

As I got out of the car, Potter leaned across and uttered yet again the theme he had repeated many times during the day: 'If there's the slightest doubt about Dobell being delivered safe and sound, we abort the thing... Houghton... you understand?'

I nodded and trudged away. I climbed the metal steps of that narrow footbridge rather more easily than I had done the first time. My rotten leg, although stiff, was functioning better. On the other hand, my responsibilities were considerably greater; the shopping bag I was swinging over my left arm contained a fortune in currency negotiable on anybody's territory.

Chapter 20

A T ANOTHER TIME, the well-lit café-bar of *Le Refuge* coming into view through the dark cluster of trees at that isolated spot would have cheered the heart of any traveller arriving on foot or by boat. And no doubt some fine bargains have been struck across the crude candle-lit rustic tables on the leafy terrace.

None of that, however, stirred me much this evening. It was not only the frightening responsibility of deciding whether or not to hand over a huge ransom in bizarre circumstances with no properly verified guarantee yet that the hostage could be released unharmed, but also the owner of the café had taken an unaccountable dislike to me. There were also sundry forces skulking in the surrounding undergrowth whose attitude, at best, was uncertain. What Counsellor Tan himself really thought of me I couldn't tell but at least he had asked me to come again. By and large I thought I was earning my money.

There were no customers outside and only two of the terrace tables were graced by candles. I avoided both of these and sat by the river in as much gloom as I could find. It was still a few minutes before nine o'clock.

A faint murmur of voices drifted across from the cabin-like bar; huge, grotesque shadows played intermittently across the gravelled terrace with every little movement of those in the café. High above, a brief funnel of noise announced the passage of a jet in the night sky. When it had gone, the distant voices in the café seemed clearer, but immediately around me settled a strange cordon of silence.

This was the ideal moment for a cigarette. In fact there was no real reason why I should not light up; I wasn't in theory hiding from anyone. But then what was I doing sitting there in the blackest part of the terrace, rather than at one of the two romantic candle-spangled rustic tables? Embarrassed by this sudden perception of my lack of logic, I contented myself with listening to the delicate plops of small night-lively fish leaping from the water down on my left. It may not have been frolicking at all, of course; perhaps they were just fed up with the pollution or the presence of some marauding pike in the depths.

The café door opened in a shaft of light, which just nicely played onto me sitting glumly by the riverside. It was the marauding pike-*patron* himself who came down the steps. He walked to within five or six yards of me.

'There's a message inside for you,' he said shortly and turned to go back.

I was suddenly very annoyed indeed with this surly cuss who seemed to bear me such a grudge.

'Let the message come out here,' I snapped, staying seated. He paused very slightly, looked over his shoulder and said very precisely: 'It is the telephone...'

I took one or two deep breaths, left my annoyance where it was and gathered up my belongings – namely, one plastic carrier bag. I had never let go of the other item of note, which was a comforting weight in the right pocket of my raincoat.

Going through the door of the café, I noticed first some faces that had been present last night and, second, that the telephone in the counter was complete with the headpiece in position. So there was no incoming call. I remained by the door.

'Which telephone?' I said to the *patron* who had already gone round the behind the bar to make up for lost time. 'Over there...' he replied, pointing to a half-partitioned cubicle at one end of the room. It was a sort of lovers' nook in an otherwise hearty 'share-everything' atmosphere, apart from the terrace, of course. I supposed there might have been another telephone in the cubicle – a 'hot-line' perhaps. Nerves out like tentacles, I brushed through the small convivial crowd who were on the best of terms with the *patron*.

Looking into the miniature railway compartment gave me the first real surprise of the evening. Counsellor Tan was sitting there, his eyes darting to the plastic bag before he stood up. Yes, he stood up to greet me.

'I thought you said I wouldn't be seeing you again,' I said sourly. We both sat down and eyed one another across a tiny table clamped to the floor.

'One mistake would be a disaster,' he said, stretching out a hand. 'May I look...?'

My right hand stayed in my pocket while I passed him the bag, He made a spot check on half a dozen different bundles. He knew anyway that we couldn't possibly have supplied that number of quality forged notes in two currencies in so short a time. He wasn't even counting of course, with his long, delicate-looking and cared-for fingers, but his abacus-mind no doubt got the feel of it all. No, he was just making sure it wasn't toilet paper.

He looked up with no emotion in his face. 'That seems all right... Please put the whole package in this.' He held up another plastic sheet of something. It was bright yellow. As he shook the folds out, we had before us yet another bag, also with a sliding clip at the top.

'You put it in,' I said without moving, 'And anyway the first bag is guaranteed to keep the moths out – why—'

'You may have an unnecessary gun in your pocket,' Tan interrupted quickly, 'but I doubt that you are also carrying a bright yellow bag filled with old newspapers – not a *yellow* bag anyway... A substitution trick would be a catastrophe for all of us.' He didn't smile even then. He just fed one bag into the other before my eyes. It was horrifying. Where were the good, clean-cut Chinese communists of old who were at least predictably honest with their nonsense? This shrewd, double-dealing character with unreasonable foresight – a mere 'dissident' – was running rings round us. And I was the maypole.

Then he pushed the now colourful container across the table towards me: 'There you are,' Counsellor Tan said coolly with a fine grasp of English idiom, even if the accent was a little too precise,

I stared at him wide-eyed. What was wrong? Had he sensed the presence of strangers who were no doubt swarming around in the shrubbery outside and was backing out?

'What's the matter?' I said in alarm. 'It's good money. Where's Dobell?'

Tan stood up. 'Wait here, with the bag' he said, 'I will tell you what to do after you have spoken with Mr Dobell.' As he left the cubicle he added: 'You are now observed... Don't try to communicate with anybody or it is finished!' He slid away into the smoky haze like Hamlet's father.

Five minutes went by. I couldn't even ask for a drink. It might count as 'communicating' with somebody; in any case I had no wish to tangle with the hostile, solid-looking *patron*. I leaned forward to peer round the edge of the compartment. He was rinsing glasses and taking his turn on the game tray. The photographs on the rear wall caught my eye again and a small idea gathered momentum in the back of my mind. It would explain the *patron*'s deference and friendliness to Tan whom he couldn't possibly have known for more than a few days; and it was only a short stop to speculate why I was so unpopular, Unfortunately, whether my theory was right or wrong did not affect the problem of getting Dobell released,

Suddenly the ringing of the telephone switched my imagination in another direction. It was about twenty minutes since Tan had left.

'It is Monsieur Tan for you...' The *patron* appeared briefly in front of the cubicle and then returned to the bar to tot up someone's bill.

I left the yellow bag on the floor by the table where I could still see it and went to the counter. I picked up the receiver with my left hand, but before answering I surveyed the company. Of the nine or ten customers, only one looked a possible interloper. He was sitting on a stool at the other end of the bar, a little apart from the rest, reading the sports weekly, *L'Equipe*. Tinted glasses, close-cropped hair and a half-length waterproof car coat with big pockets – yes, that would be one of Grillon's DST lot. Then he moved slightly and I saw his crutches leaning against the bar. He had only one leg.

'Lawson,' I said into the mouthpiece.

'Take the river path from the terrace and thirty yards down from the café you will find a small rowing dinghy moored at the bank,' said Counsellor Tan. 'Just drop the bag into the boat... And remember you will be watched all the way.'

'Where's Dobell?' I said. 'I do nothing until—'

'Wait…' There was a pause and clattering in the earpiece as the receiver at the other end knocked against something. I heard some quick breathing for a few seconds and then:

'Ken… It's Henry Dobell…' The voice was weak and full of fatigue. I felt my face tighten and I must have gone very pale. I let the bar take my weight.

'Yes – it's all right. Henry, it's all right! Don't worry – it's almost over!' My own voice sounded odd, too. 'Where are you?' I added quickly.

'I don't know – I'm tied up…' Dobell's voice was cut off. Then Tan spoke.

'He is going to signal to show you where he is… But first, Mr Lawson, you have understood, haven't you?'

'Yes!' I shouted. 'For God's sake get on—'

'Look out of the café windows across the river and you will see the lights of a four-storey apartment block to the right and on a rise… It is about three hundred yards from where you are.' The Chinese spoke in a clipped, exact way. I recognised the place immediately. 'All right…' Another slight pause and then it was Dobell speaking:

'I'm propped against a wall, Ken… They want me to turn a switch on and off three times – you must watch the building.'

Immediately at the very end of the top floor, a room light flashed in a window three times. Then it remained dark. I already believed it but I asked for more.

'Henry, do it again – twice!'

Again the room was lit twice in quick succession. Dobell's strained, tired voice spoke to me once more. 'Ken …'

'Yes?'

'If it's been agreed, this isn't the time to mess around... I am unharmed so far, but there's a gun at my head.'

A few faint noises on the line ended in a click as the receiver was replaced.

There was no conscious decision to be made. Henry Dobell was three hundred yards away, unharmed on his own admission and I was no longer thinking in terms of a 'choice'. As soon as I had heard Dobell's voice any idea of 'aborting', to use Potter's term, vanished.

I picked up the plastic bag and headed for the door. On the way, I looked hard at the *patron* who responded with the expression of granite defiance that I had come to know so well. 'As an Indochina *ancien combattant*, you ought to know the difference between a Vietnamese and a Chinese...' I said quietly in passing.

Some nearby conversation stopped suddenly and heads looked up. The *patron* said nothing but he watched me all the way to the door. As I went out, I turned to see him still staring, but there was now a strange look in his eyes.

I walked quickly across the terrace and down the steps to the footpath along the river bank. I found the boat tied up against a post opposite which was a rough path leading up into the trees; I guessed that this was the way Tan had come down from the busy track last night.

The boat was a tiny eight foot skiff which would usually be paddled or poled along. It was only this which made me hesitate a few seconds. I just couldn't see the purpose of choosing half a punt as the receptacle for £400,000. The dinghy obviously couldn't go anywhere worthwhile with a paddle or a piece of stick – even supposing a very talented boatman surged up out of the darkness ready to try. Finally, I leaned over carefully and dropped the bag into the bottom of the boat. With the soft thud of the package against the floorboards, the very light craft began to rock gently.

Before I had even straightened up, an outboard motor coughed into life some thirty or forty yards downstream and at the same time there was a sudden whip-like slashing noise and the dripping of water. Against the reflected light on the surface of the river I could just see a pencil line of rope stretched tight from the bows of the skiff. The small craft took off almost with the *élan* of a water-skier's dry-start.

I turned and ran awkwardly back along the footpath towards the bridge on which Potter was waiting.

'He's there!' I said, panting and waving excitedly at the small block of apartments. 'Top floor – last room on the right.'

We clambered into the Peugeot and Potter raced it along the track until we found a way up. It could only have taken a couple of minutes.

There was only one central stairway to the building. Potter dashed ahead. He seemed to go up a flight at a time. I had just left the second floor when I heard Potter hammering on a door and shouting Dobell's name. 'The skiff was already on tow!' I called out, trying to finish a conversation we had been having in the car. A door was flung open somewhere below and a voice yelled the equivalent of 'Belt up, you noisy bastards!'

I found Potter who was still thumping on the door of the apartment occupied by 'Monsieur J. Lemaitre', according to a small, plaque under the bell-push.

Potter tried kicking the lock until he hurt his foot. I

pulled him away and, before he could interfere, I lined up the Browning at an angle against the lock so that, with luck, the round would embed in the wall rather than go ricocheting round the room.

I fired and the noise was appalling in that confined space of echoing brickwork. A whole panel of the door had split with the impact and the lock looked as if it had been dynamited. This time one kick from Potter was enough and the door almost came off the hinges. I noticed now that he also had a gun in his hand. I found the light switch and turned it on.

He was lying in the far side of the room trussed up generously with medical tape. He was gagged and blindfolded in the same way. I rushed across and tore the taping from his face.

But it was not Henry Dobell. Instead the homely-looking Monsieur Lemaitre stared at us from the level of his own carpet, eyes bulging, and dumb with terror.

Chapter 21

THIS TIME a real decision was called for. I made it an instant before Potter could react to what I was doing. I wheeled round and snatched the automatic from his hand.

'Car keys!' I snapped. Potter glared at me, breathing hard and fingering his spectacles.

'What are you playing at now?' he said with unreasonable calm.

'I'm going after the money! Now, quick – keys!'

'Don't be a fool, Ken – I'll back you up... it's not your fault.'

'You know as well as I do that it's just the turn of events Houghton has been waiting for – I've lost the money without getting Dobell. And I happen to want to see my hacienda again! Now... Keys!'

'They're in the car.'

'Ian, I swear I'll put a bullet through one of your great big feet – *give me the keys!*'

He gave them to me.

'By the way,' I said, moving towards the door, 'I think Tan passed himself off as a Vietnamese at Le Refuge. The *patron* evidently has some bad memories of Indochina and Tan must have got his cooperation with a cock and bull story somehow involving innocent me.'

Potter didn't reply. He was already trying to disentangle Monsieur Lemaitre from the rest of the tape bindings and at whom he was firing unanswered questions. It was a pity, as I was to learn later, that Potter had not taken more interest in my Indochinese guesswork; it wasn't the whole truth by a long way, but if

Potter had followed it up, things might have turned out differently.

'Take the plasticine from his ears and then he'll be able to hear you,' I said and rushed to the stairs. As I passed the different levels, people all over the place disappeared like rabbits into their burrows. As we have noted already, the Browning 9 mm is an intimidating weapon and never more than when being waved around by a man with a wild look in his eye.

The Peugeot bumped and slid crazily along the rutted track which followed the river course. With an unfamiliar driver at the wheel, the car was often largely out of control. The risks I was taking were a direct reflection of the desperate situation in which I found myself.

There seemed to be little choice of actually recovering the money and I was giving chase chiefly for the form of the thing; a sort of last gesture to show that I had *tried* in this ill-fated assignment. No, I really needed the car to give me a head start before Potter felt obliged to sound the alarm. I thought, too, that he might delay that as long as he could; Potter was a decent sort really.

The *Ile de le Déviation* was by now far behind and the river has spread to its proper width. For the last half a mile or so, the course had been almost straight, I was on the point of giving up the pathetic search when, through the open driver's window, I heard something that caused me to stop immediately. I cut the engine and jumped out.

The noise of an outboard motor sent me running a few yards ahead to a gap in the bushes where there was a better view of the water. Perhaps sixty yards further on, well in the centre of the river, I could just make out a small boat moving slowly downstream. I scarcely believed it even then. It could have been any outboard on a late evening cruise. But that one did look as if it might be towing something.

I ran back and took the car another two or three hundred yards along the track and stopped again. From a new vantage point on the bank, I watched and waited as the boat whined nearer.

When it was almost abreast, I could see that there was indeed a tiny dinghy behind it that just had to be the tiny punt-skiff. This had now been pulled up on a short rope. In my excitement I found myself saying aloud: 'Well, lucky Lawson, after all!' However, what to do about this marvellous bit of luck was another matter.

Three hundred years away downstream was a bridge lined with street-lamps that carried a major road across the river – as the lights of passing cars showed. A view from the bridge, for a start, seemed a good idea.

I drove at a safe pace to a point just before the bridge and then up a side track, which curled round steeply to join the main road above. I stopped the car on the verge at the top and walked quickly towards the middle of the bridge.

A group of men with a particular bearing about them were leaning against the concrete parapet of the bridge; they were looking intently upstream at the on-coming launch still a hundred yards away. At the other side of the bridge was parked a black Renault 16 complete with driver and radio mast. They must have been following the boat along the river bank and had also decided that a view from the bridge was too good to miss.

A happy thought was that although Potter had said that they would not 'interfere', this French Special Services squad almost certainly *would* have done so if anything untoward had been observed since they left the island. Nobody seemed that excited and probably therefore nothing had happened, which meant that the yellow bag would be intact. In the circumstances, Potter would forgive me for borrowing his official car.

The knot of French security police were too preoccupied watching the approaching convoy to bother about me. So I waited like the curious bystanders – of which there were a handful not wanting to miss what other people were looking at.

Then one of the DST men suddenly pointed and said loudly: 'He's heading straight for the pillar!'

The bridge was supported in the middle by a single concrete column of massive girth, and impending collision was clear for all to see. A young man with his arm around his enchanted *petite amie* shouted, 'Hey! Wake up – steer away!'

Then other pedestrians joined in with whistles and raucous calls and rude laughter. But I noticed that the DST men kept silent. They were not interfering.

The scruffy little launch had a half-enclosed windshield and we couldn't see the pilot. However, from twenty yards away, I did notice, in the bottom of the skiff on tow, a package that glistened in the lights from the bridge – in the manner of a yellow plastic bag.

I was smiling broadly for a moment – as were most of the other spectators – but for quite different reasons.

A few seconds of fascinated silence preceded a heavy echoing thud. The boat was not moving fast enough to do much damage, but the crunch, when it came, followed immediately by erratic whining of the motor was dramatic enough for the onlookers, and satisfying. The skiff swung round with the current and its own momentum to bang against the launch broadside on.

'*Putain* – there's *no* pilot!'

'Get down there then!'

One man started to climb over the parapet and onto the column itself where metal brackets provided convenient footholds. The one who had spoken last with the orders turned to the gallery: 'This is police business – move away please!'

Nobody took any notice; they never do in France until the teargas grenades are heaved around.

But I scurried off to collect Potter's car, which I then drove back to the crowd in the middle of the bridge. The senior DST man peered at the diplomatic plates and then looked at me with no sign of recognition as I got out.

'That's my shopping bag in the skiff,' I said, looking down. The man in the boat was crouching down over the engine, which was still burbling and sparking at the interference. 'My name is Lawson,' I added, '… from London… er… Monsieur Potter works for me.' My argument didn't have its full potential impact because of a conversation going on between the boat and the parapet:

'But the throttle's been jammed open, I tell you!'

'Give it full choke – that will stop it.'

'There's no choke on these things.'

'Of course there is – look at the tit under the throttle linkage.'

The man who had been half-listening to me turned round impatiently and called down, 'Pull the fuel lead from the tank – you don't have to play at being mechanics!' He returned to me and it seemed from his manner that he was not inclined to be helpful.

'Look,' I said, 'you saw me put the bag in the skiff earlier – what's the problem?'

He still wasn't going to admit anything but he shouted down to the engineer, 'Throw us that bag, Michel!'

The yellow package arrived on the parapet. It was dripping wet and the sliding clip had not completely sealed the top. Despite the irrepressible hopes born during the last fifteen minutes or so, the awful doubt that had never been far away now surged up inside me. It left me coldly detached and feeling a little sick.

'Open it, if you like,' I enjoined. Down below the motor spluttered and stopped.

'I found it!' called a triumphant voice. At this, the hard-faced thirty-five-year-old standing with me half turned to launch an instant insult but curiosity won the day and he pulled his attention back to me. He slipped the clip back and in the bag we saw several weeks' supply of neatly folded newspapers. Some of the bundles were sodden but the rest were dry. All were of good quality – scores of old copies of *Le Monde*, in fact. I managed a sickly grin.

'On second thoughts, perhaps you would be good enough to give the bag to Monsieur Potter when you next see him.'

I motored quietly away and soon found a road with a big sign that read, 'Direction PARIS.'

Forty-five minutes later, after an uneventful and thoughtful drive, I stopped the Peugeot immediately opposite the British Embassy building in the *rue du faubourg St Honoré* in the heart of the city. During the day, parking in that traffic-cluttered street is a matter of naked aggression, but at night-time the area is almost deserted, so I put the car in a meter bay at exactly 1.15 am.

Potter's Browning I placed under the driver's seat where, if he had any sense of continuity, he would find it immediately. I locked up and put the keys in an envelope containing insurance documents that I had found in the glove-locker. I then dropped the envelope in the Embassy mailbox. A neat, ordered end to a wild evening.

I had nowhere to go and, all things considered, I certainly didn't want to compromise any friends in Paris by seeking shelter.

There is only one way for a foreigner to spend a night in a French hotel without leaving official traces and that is to be invited to do so by a lady who has your interests at heart for the evening. It can be expensive and the more you pay for comfort and other advantages, the easier it becomes to forget the essential sordidness of it all.

With very little ready money in my pocket, it seemed that I was due to plumb the depths of sordidness, I walked towards a relevant district.

I had barely turned the corner when a small car passed and slowed to a crawl just ahead. A blonde head leaned out of the window, looking back and waiting for me to catch up. There's quite an army of girls in circulation in the streets of Paris looking for customers in the way – although this was not a favoured area of the city. Moreover, I didn't think the loose change in my pocket was going to get me very far in this style of operation. But I walked over to negotiate anyway.

As I approached, the driver addressed me in English – with a charming German accent:

'Perhaps we could have an exchange of views, Mr Lawson…' Christel Scholze brushed some strands of blonde hair from her face and smiled at me.

Frankly, I wanted to run to the nearest church or to

the British Embassy – whichever I could reach first. Christel was still smiling. I stared, immobile, for some seconds while all sorts of possibilities struggled for recognition in my mind.

Then, without a word, I walked round to the passenger door and got into the car.

Whatever kind of frightening new problems this might bring, at least it solved the present one of getting me off the streets for a while.

Chapter 22

WITH LITTLE OTHER traffic at that time of night, in ten minutes we had arrived in a sombre district near the Citroen factories in a sombre south-west corner of Paris.

There had not been much conversation on the way and I had even refrained from asking where we were going. It seemed of little importance. I just let it happen.

A sudden turn into a side street and almost immediately, outside an apartment block of boring appearance, the little Simca swung off the road and boomed down a ramp into the faintly chemical smells of an underground parking lot.

Echoing steps across the concrete floor, then into a 'Maximum load 3 people' small lift, which took us up to the fifth floor. Three paces to the right, fumbling with the key in the lock accompanied by a soft, feminine curse and then the door opened. Christel Scholze went into the darkened room, switched on a table-lamp and turned to me standing by the door, full of apprehension.

'Come in,' she said with a nice smile. 'Make yourself at home...'

It was a modest, sparsely furnished little apartment with a bathroom attached, In England, it would probably be called a 'bedsitter'; in France, for some reason, these places are called 'studios'.

'Who does it belong to?' I asked, closing the door behind me.

'Me, for the time being...' Another big smile. It was perfectly clear who, in principle, was paying the rent. Fraulein Scholze busied herself in a small alcove-kitchenette and then called out, 'You can have vodka or hot chocolate – there doesn't seem to be much else.'

That interrupted my chain of thought for a moment. 'What about both,' I suggested. 'We might make history.'

'Okay!' There was a soft musical chuckle from behind a piece of plastic sheeting that served to define the kitchen area.

I went to the small window that overlooked the street, pushed it open wider and breathed deeply in the cool right air. Below were two lines of parked cars; opposite was some office building with a forgotten light or two burning in the interior. It was all silent, peaceful and a long way from the *Ile de la Déviation*,

Christel emerged from her hostess labours bringing a tray on which were two mugs of hot chocolate, two small glasses and a three-quarter full bottle of ice-cold vodka. She put the lot down on a small table. Since it was a bedsitter, we sat on the bed. The refreshments were within easy reach.

'Well, how is your investigation going?' she asked, clinking glasses.

'Fine...' I said, '... as you must have noticed.'

Christel exchanged her dose of firewater for a mug of the other, more gentle, sleeping-draught mixture.

'Your two meetings with Tan were... were noted,' she agreed, with some reluctance. She looked into the chocolate brew, delicately pulling aside with her little finger the milk-skin that had formed at the top. Her face turned to me expectantly – encouraging me to add some personal reminiscences for the record. I wondered just how much the Russian surveillance had provided.

'Anyway, it's all irrelevant,' I said topping up the glasses from the USSR's subversive bottle, 'I have retired from the case.'

Although there was a slight pause in the dialogue, my news provoked no dramatic reaction. 'Why – what do you mean?' said Christel evenly.

'I mean that my "investigation"—' (I rolled some irony into the word) — 'is finished, because there are certain aspects I don't much like... notably being beaten up fairly regularly.'

Christel pulled a face, and put her mug down quickly and turned towards me with that sympathetic 'oh-ing' noise that is so often delivered sarcastically. Perhaps it was the vodka, but any sarcasm went over my head.

She slipped an arm over my shoulder and her hand just did light things on the fabric of my shirt. There are some women who know how to touch a man anywhere; and there are others who mess it up even when attending to places obviously designated for the purpose, I was in the grip of the former and I held on very tightly with both hands to my mug of chocolate.

'So I really have no views to offer in exchanges,' I mused. 'I'm sorry to disappoint you...'

'Well, that is not exactly why I came after you tonight—'

'Where is the rest of the team?'

Christel picked up her glass and drank half the shot of vodka at once. Her eyes downcast, examining the remains, she said, 'They are occupied with Tan, of course. He has been watched continuously since we found him with Dobell in Bangkok.' She paused and looked at me again. 'What did Tan say?' It was the £400,000 question.

'He posed certain conditions for Dobell's release, which I considered unacceptable, but no doubt negotiations will continue with another party,'

Christel had an odd expression on her face, but I wasn't sure whether she knew I was lying or not.

The sound of a car arriving in the street below caught my attention. I gently disengaged the slim, very suntanned and knowledgeable hand from my shoulder and went over to the window again. A neat, open sports car had stopped, motor still running, in the middle of the quiet street. The young couple in the car were having a furious argument and their voices echoed off the tall, silent buildings. As I turned away, the car door slammed and any hopes of romance dissolved in an exasperated noise of fierce acceleration, followed by quick, tripping steps in the street. Then quiet again.

It seemed to me that, doubtless with nothing like that frustrated young fellow's charm, and certainly lacking his knock-me-over sports car, I would he blighted for ever if I turned my back on smiling fortune up here on the fifth floor behind the Citroen Works. And with no offence to the young lady who had just scuttled home, I was quite sure that Christel Scholze had a great deal more to offer than her. I had seen most of it in Bangkok.

'I didn't finish telling you why I picked you up tonight,' Christel was saying. The tone was casual but we seemed now to be sitting even closer on the comfortable bed. 'Go on,' I said, forcing a sceptical note into my voice.

'Two reasons,' she said softly. 'I am really very sorry about your leg...' There was that nice, head-reeling Lanvin confection wafting around again. And, because it didn't belong to me, instinctively I started to fondle a long lock of real blonde hair which somehow seemed to be falling over my shoulder. Then there was a gentle –

and no doubt apologetic – hand on my knee making small amends. A minute or two passed.

'It was the other leg,' I said.

Christel suddenly swung round and down onto the floor very close in front of me. From there she was able to work on both my knees with doubly exciting results, while I looked down into a face that wasn't quite beautiful but attractive and, above all, full of character.

From this angle and dizzy height, too, the low scoop of the cotton dress revealed a lot of her well-shaped, young-looking breasts; she had a slim, gymnast's figure. I was beginning to feel very hot and bothered.

'What was the second reason?' I asked, Christel lowered her eyes again and edged up a little nearer. A profoundly disturbing soft warmth was now being transferred to the inside of my sensitive knees.

'You could have made a lot of trouble for me in Bangkok… I would not have enjoyed being arrested by the Thais. But you didn't... and one good turn deserves another.' A small, knowing smile played around her mouth.

'I just didn't have time to see about it,' I said.

She pressed one fingernail hard into my trouser log with affected annoyance. It was exquisite. What an admission! No doubt a tiny something of what those unfortunates feel who enjoy being lashed around by their partners with leather thongs. No, surely not – I was merely being anaesthetised by the vodka.

'How long can I stay?' I said. 'It might suit me to keep my head down for a few days ...'

Christel looked genuinely pleased. 'As long as I'm around!' she said with some enthusiasm. 'What I do here is my own business.' She gave my knees a reassuring squeeze, meaning 'I'll be back in a jiffy,' and then retired to the bathroom.

I slumped back on the bad, very thoughtful. That I was being lodged in a Russian 'safe-house' was obvious and I scarcely believed that Christel, for all her charming 'regrets', had brought me there solely on her own initiative. Moreover, they wouldn't be 'blowing' one of their hideaways to me for no reason at all.

I had no wish to be interrupted in bed with this desirable lithe-limbed girl by some grubby characters knocking down the door with their flashlight cameras or to be confronted later by a record of events from some system already installed in the premises. It was not that I feared being 'compromised' – it was too late for all that and they could send photographs to squalid magazines all round the world, to Charles Houghton or make picture postcards for all I cared. *A la rigueur*, they could even think in terms of Evelyn back in Mexico where, after the row, peace would be restored overnight. Perhaps. No, I just didn't like the idea of my privacy being invaded and I happen to be square and prudish enough to believe that bed is a private place, especially where two people are concerned.

A thin line of light showed under the bathroom door. The noise of running water stopped with the squeak of a worn tap. Then shortly after, the light went out. But the door remained shut.

I sat up straight, watching. Some seconds passed and then the line of light appeared again three or four times in quick succession. It seemed to be the night of the year for playing with light switches. I sighed and suddenly felt vary weary. A moment later, Christel came out carrying some clothes over her arm.

She was wearing a knee-length white dressing-gown made of some light material; the simple garment itself had no particular 'allure'; it was the way it was worn and what was inside that was so dangerous. She came to sit down again and filled the glasses on the way.

'Thanks,' I said. 'This must be the last – I'm almost asleep.

Christel grinned at me cheerfully and wrinkled her sun-freckled nose, but she didn't say anything. I stood up and pointed to a rather narrow divan bench-seat under the window. 'Am I allowed to kip down there?'

A slight pause, which may have indicated surprise, but that was all.

'Of course you can – but you don't *have* to be uncomfortable, you know…' It was a pleasant, unfussed remark. I mumbled something again about being tired to which Christel replied gently: 'Yes, I suppose you are.' Her 'understanding' was unexpected and that troubled me a little.

Within five minutes, I was reclining on the makeshift bed, shoes off, but still dressed. Christel found a spare blanket in a drawer somewhere and gave it to me. She turned her bedside lamp off and threw the dressing-gown on the bottom of the bed.

And, masochist that I am, I was watching as bottled-up light in the room or from outside played on her supple textbook body for an instant before she disappeared between the sheets. A soft 'goodnight' all round and that was that. Except for Christel's quiet, last-minute and good-humoured effort: 'If you change your mind, I don't mind being woken up.'

Nobody came bursting in during the next few hours but despite my real fatigue, I hardly slept at all. At every small sound in the building or from the street I was wide awake. And even in that semi-conscious 'dozing' state, my mind was juggling with theories mixed up with a repeated dream sequence in which I saw bargemen pulling from the river a large yellow sack containing Dobell's body. Variations on the vengeance theme kept running through my head – the personal crusade I was going to wage against Tan, however long it took, and then there was Houghton. Had he accidentally saved my life with that malfunctioning gun turned against me? Or had he hoped to have me killed by deliberately providing a weapon for self-defence which didn't work? Potter knew something – or guessed. Had he not tried to warn me? I fidgeted and plotted for hours...

Christel had fallen asleep within twenty minutes; it seemed that she could dispose of her conscience as easily as her clothes. The soft noise of her regular breathing made me cross. Once even, I got up and padded across to look at her. She was only partly covered and this did me no good at all so I crept miserably back to the bench to chew some more on my blanket.

I must have slept for a couple of hours very late. Suddenly I saw the small table by my head and Christel bending over with a cup of coffee. She was dressed and cheerful. 'It's eight o'clock,' she said. 'I have to go out now but you take your time... I will be back later in the morning.' A wide spring-like smile.

I swung my legs onto the floor and sipped at the coffee appreciatively. 'Well, I need a little time to work things out,' I said. Christel studied me for a second.

'I assume that "keeping your head down" for a while has something to do with a bag of old newspapers in place of the ransom money...?' she said carefully.

I held my head in my hands. It is of course a fine interrogation technique to fire tricky questions when the victim's responses are at low ebb. I couldn't even muster enough defiance to ask how she knew about that; but it wasn't difficult to guess.

'I just want to go home – to Mexico,' I said wearily. And there are a number of people who are going to try to stop me.'

'Stay here and think about it,' she said in a reassuring tone. 'There's no problem – nobody knows you are here.'

That immediately injected some fight and spirit into dejected Lawson; I do clown about a bit, but just what kind of a fool did she take me for?

'I suppose that was "nobody" you were signalling to with the bathroom light a few hours ago?'

Christel's eyes widened and her mouth dropped open. She looked almost frightened, I blundered on sarcastically. 'And what happened to the comrades – I was waiting for them all night!'

For the first time in our brief acquaintance, Christel Scholze looked utterly confused. Under her suntan she was blushing deeply. She picked up her handbag and walked slowly towards the door. She turned to face me and stood with her long brown legs slightly apart in the 'at ease' position with both hands holding the handbag hanging down like a sporran.

'Yes, I lied,' she said quietly. 'They know you are here of course. But my signal last night meant that there was no reason to… to continue!' Christel hesitated. I gaped at her, in my turn – dumbfounded. 'In other words, I didn't want us to be disturbed!' she blurted out.

She banged the door on leaving.

I had never really believed the films and theatre

where people go on staring dramatically at doors long after others have left. I can now describe every square inch of that door of a fifth-floor apartment in a building behind the Citroen Works.

Chapter 23

TWO HOURS WAS enough to disguise and, in part, overtake the effects of a disastrous night. The shower worked noisily, with the pipes in the wall throbbing ominously and an electric razor had already been thoughtfully plugged into a socket somewhere behind the medicine chest. A brand-new toothbrush encased in plastic awaited a test-run on my vodka-rimed teeth and there were a number of *après-douche* sweet-smelling things in bottles that I avoided.

By 10.30 am I had finished a second mug of coffee and completed a preliminary round of unlikely escape planning - not primarily from Christel's tender care, of course, but rather from France and Europe in general. This involved the telephone and although there was one in the apartment, it was obviously wise not to touch it.

I scribbled a note in Spanish meaning, 'Back in ten minutes' and left it on the table. There was no particular reason to write in Spanish, but then there was no good reason for me to be in the apartment in the first place.

I had just finished, after several unsuccessful efforts, jamming the door closed from outside with a small wad of paper, when the lift arrived. Christel stepped out and took my arm. 'I've got news for you!' she said excitedly. I pushed the door open for her, retrieved the carefully fashioned wedge and followed her inside.

'What's this?' she asked.

'A note to the plumber. What's the news?'

'Tan left at 8.10 this morning on a Varig flight to Caracas!'

We both sat again on the ever-ready bed. 'It can't be

true,' I said. 'Venezuela doesn't have relations with Peking – he won't be allowed to disembark.'

'He left Orly on a South Vietnamese passport in the name of Tanh Thi Quang...'

I stared at Christel for a moment and then I laughed. I was thinking of my earlier purely coincidental conclusion that Tan had claimed – for different reasons – to be a Vietnamese to the *patron* of Le Refuge.

'No – it's true!' exclaimed Christel, misunderstanding my reaction.

'Yes, perhaps it is... How do you know?' After ten in the morning a modest awareness of events creeps into my metabolism and I am able to ask simple questions.

'Oh, we're not short of informants at Orly,' she said airily. 'But I've done a deal on your behalf!' she added and kissed my fresh-shaven, clean-smelling right cheek, as if to remind me of what I had missed last night. I recoiled not from the contact, but from the alarming statement.

'What sort of deal?'

'We will get you out of France if you go after Tan in Venezuela – you are well-placed to do it and we can't move so easily there...'

I couldn't believe it. The Russians offering *me* a job? Still, it was true that for the moment I didn't have any other.

'How can you move me out?' I asked. 'At any normal air or sea exit point, I could be picked up just like that...' I flicked my fingers and, with this gesture, it occurred to me that there was still a little vodka left in the bottle. It seemed that an appropriate moment to finish it was almost upon us. Christel waited until I filled the two glasses. 'You will be given Russian papers,' she said.

'We go to Havana first... After which you use your own passport'

'Havana?' I muttered stupidly. 'That's Cuba...' Henry Dobell had spent a long time in Cuba. A number of frightening ideas flitted through my head at this point but finally one issue was uppermost in my thoughts. Cuba was very much closer to Mexico than France was. In any case, the prospect of leaving Paris disguised as a Russian appealed to my artistic sense and it was a lot more plausible than the fantastic escape themes I had been toying with.

The surprising Christel and I knocked back our vodka tots. I was the only one who coughed.

*

Forty-eight hours later we were high over the Atlantic. I was in the company of a saturnine Soviet official in his late thirties. I didn't even know his surname, nor whether he was from the Embassy in Paris or elsewhere, But he enjoyed a diplomatic passport and had shepherded me through Customs and Immigration at Orly with great aplomb.

I had a passport which I couldn't read, an unusual hat and a pair of dark glasses. Christel had been at the back of the queue boarding the same flight, but what her status was I didn't know.

During a couple of visits to the lavatory at the back of the aircraft, I passed Christel who looked up both times with exactly the same expression of bland non-recognition,

My Russian travelling companion – Youri was his Christian name, he confided – apart from his rich native tongue, spoke only Spanish. Which was an embarrassment to both of us since I had exhausted all the Spanish I knew in the note left in Christel's studio. But he did drink and he did play chess. He took me to the cleaners four times in succession. None of Ian Potter's ill considered Philidor's Mates – we were now operating at the level of the Pawn and Bishop's Lay-off. Anybody who knows what that means scarcely needs bother to read on.

I was fascinated by Youri's hands. They were not all that pretty; it was just that there were large rocklike corns on the third knuckle of the middle fingers and the back edge of each hand had been sharpened into a hard callous. Yes, I made a poor showing. Well, my friends, have *you* ever tried playing chess with someone who has home-grown knuckledusters?

As we dipped down over the Caribbean Sea, I had come to one conclusion to my satisfaction, however: Christel Scholze, or whatever her real name was, was a great deal more important in the KGB hierarchy than 'just part of the surveillance team' – as she claimed earlier.

Chapter 24

W E STAYED for one night in Havana, very much in transit, in a severe hotel. The Russian gorilla was in the room next to mine. Christel apparently had separate arrangements elsewhere. The only thing I saw of Havana was the road to Jose Marti airport. And I was happy to see it again the next day when Christel came to the hotel to say that we were leaving on a flight to Caracas that morning.

Youri, the swarthy Ukrainian, accompanied me as far as the rather military looking Immigration section where he handed me my own British passport (confiscated the day before, along with the Russian one) duly stamped with a Cuban twenty-four-hour transit visa. I felt almost human again. Youri smiled thinly and offered his hand in farewell. It was like shaking hands with a shovel.

Touching down at Maiquetía Airport in Caracas was a special occasion for me. Whatever the aircraft and no matter whose it is, when the machine arrives on the tarmac in an ordered way, I always feel that I have got away with something. The other reason for my joy in actually reaching Venezuela was that there was now nothing, in theory, to stop me walking from the Customs desk straight onto a flight for Mexico City. Blonde Christel, it was true, was there in the colourful background, still studiously ignoring me; but if I chose to go and buy an onward ticket to Mexico, she could scarcely stop me.

But I did as I was told, as psychologist Scholze knew I would. And there was nothing difficult about it, particularly as the initial arrangements called for my installation in the Hotel Tamanaco. This rather plush US tourist-orientated palace is built on a rise with a spectacular view of the city, which sits cradled in a valley formed by the counterforts of the Cordillera of the coast.

Caracas is another of the world's grotesque examples of unbalanced development, to use a neutral phrase; it has a chic and fashionable centre with elegant buildings and girdled by a superb auto-pista network scarcely adequate for the rush-hour traffic. The style and mint condition of many of the cars and cheap petrol remind you that Venezuela is a major oil-producing country. And yet only a few minutes away from the affluent centre and the green residential areas with gardened villas and mansions, the hillsides are strewn with the squalor and poverty of the tin-roofed shacks of the squatter *ranchitos*.

Since there is a Communist party in Venezuela there's not much doubt who the unfortunate *ranchitos* voted for in the last elections.

The only squatter in the Tamanaco Hotel was K. Lawson, there by the grace of the KGB and technically on the run from his own kith and kin – never mind the injustice of it all – but with a highly personal interest in the fortunes of the recently resigned Chinese diplomat, Tan, now masquerading as a Vietnamese with an 'h' on the end of his name. What exactly the Russians wanted to do with Tan, assuming that we found him, had not yet been made clear; but I rather hoped they had multiple crippling in mind, if not assassination,

For the moment my duties were simple, I was confined to the hotel by casual order of Fraulein Scholze who called me at pre-arranged times every day to bring news of the search progress. This went on for almost a week, enlivened by two false leads, both Japanese, one of whom had gone to live by the thermal fountains of San Juan De Los Morros in the mountains of Guarico. It was a long way for a Japanese to go for a hot bath.

By this time, I had worked up my poolside suntan and was becoming bored with the hotel menu. I decided to remain for the weekend and then, with or without permission, leave for Mexico. From there I would organise (with the help of Lorenzo, Evelyn's policeman uncle) my own private campaign to catch up with Counsellor Tan. I would also plot in depth the final undoing of Charles Houghton – if I could obtain confirmation that he deserved to be undone. But that was a much more difficult and long-term project.

Early Saturday afternoon after yet another hamburger lunch and several beers by the pool, I was reclining under a colourful sunshade and working through a book of easy crossword puzzles bought in the hotel kiosk. Just in front of me two long-limbed Pan Am stewardesses, propped up on their elbows, were sunning their backs; the brunette of the pair, who already had an all-over tan as far as I could see, had long hair and a sultry look which I found appealing. Just for the fun of the thing, I ogled a bit, on and off, and smiled my crooked smile, hoping to start up a friendly conversation with what would surely be a political ally.

All I got for my pains, despite the allure of a more durable colour than most in the vicinity and a leaner frame than many, was a look of blank indifference. I contented myself with the theory that she was short-sighted. This was satisfactory until the moment when she ran out of cigarettes and threw her case to one side with a charming, petulant gesture. This was the big chance. I smiled broadly and flashed my box of Bensons invitingly:

'Have one of mine…' I purred.

She certainly heard me and saw the obvious, polite expression of concern for her needs. One hand clapping a tiny bikini-top in place, she flipped over onto her back and pulled a wide-brimmed straw hat over her face. It seemed that my brand just wouldn't do. So I now had a view of a lot of unresponsive straw and, beyond that, a long, brown body glistening with suntan oil, which surely I could inspect at closer quarters – if only I had the right make of cigarettes.

What make it was I shall never know, because a second later, a lithe, mahogany-coloured male whom I had noticed prowling around the pool during the week in various brief, flashy satin swimming trunks (leopard spots it was today) was there, crouching down confidently on one knee by my coveted brunette, and engaged in a happy exchange.

Who *are* these pampered-looking drones with the winning smiles who seem to be perpetually on   holiday round the world at any beach or swimming pool worth the name? Just one or two of these beautiful young men on any given beat– spoiling it for the rest of us –darkly tanned, sporting expensive wrist-watches and as often as not a fine gold chain necklace, sunglasses of course and what little else is the best in close-fitting casual wear. They don't sit around that much – they *patrol*, slowly, frequently in pairs; they know the terrain and they are the barman's best friend.

Where do they go and what do they do when it rains? But the best of luck to them, I suppose; no doubt in the off-season they are good sons to their mothers.

Three yards away the drone with the leopard-skin

jock-strap rippled his deltoids as he settled more comfortably – and permanently – with the two enchanted American girls.

I wanted to throw one of my brown (military issue) plimsolls at him, but I feared I might not got it back. Yes, I had packed this footwear (to which I am sentimentally attached) initially with the Bangkok sun in mind. Some would say a bit of a rebel, perhaps, and I must admit to getting a kick out of arriving at a chic *plage* or poolside wearing long dark blue gym-shorts and old khaki plimsolls.

But, in case you are wondering what separates me from the exhibitionist drongos in their satin briefs is the fact that once installed within waving distance of the bar, *I don't move*, of course. Instead, people take it in turns to come up and stare at me. But I have the last laugh – especially confident in my long-life Mexican tan and the knowledge that the discriminating will immediately recognise a fine athletic body reposing there – disdainful of modern fashion aids. On the other hand, it did seem that the Tarzan G-string was making more headway with the off-duty Pan Am ladies than my PT shorts.

I sighed, sipped at my beer and turned over on my front so that the vulgar scene ahead should not disturb me further. I had a regular meeting with Christel Scholze in my room in half an hour's time. So thinking, I fell asleep in the warm Venezuelan sun.

*

An ice-cold edge of something slithering down my spine made me wake with a start. I turned and half sat up a little dizzy and blinking into the white glare of the afternoon. A familiar slender hand was using a straw to drop some chilled, fizzy liquid down my back.

'What time is it?' I said, rubbing my eyes.

On this occasion Christel did answer me. 'It is ten minutes after three and you are more than half an hour late for the meeting...'

Quite right. All I could do was to mumble 'sorry' incoherently several times because, still dazed by this rude awakening, two things were confusing me. Firstly, it was a surprise to find Christel there at all confronting me in a very public place; until then she had been so careful about our contacting arrangements.

The second aspect which was preoccupying me – and apparently a lot of other people at the poolside – was that this tall blonde, with her supple dancer's figure, looked a dream in a neat lemon-yellow bikini whose talented designer was clearly short of material. She dropped down beside me and my head reeled again.

'What are you doing here?' I grumbled. 'It's very bad security...'

'Well, you were not in your room and I didn't think the news could wait – I think we have found him!' she said cheerfully. That changed everything, except the bad security, and I sat up quickly, asking for more.

'We are almost sure... You can judge for yourself.' Christel was delving into a small straw carrier bag containing the usual support items of ladies clad in minimum swimwear.

'It was sheer luck, really. The local Party organisation had found no trace of him, but yesterday they were checking on a German who arrived a week ago and who had been living in Paraguay – they check all Germans, you know, because of the number of ex-Nazis who disappeared in this part of the world – and they discovered that an unidentified Asian had moved into a house with him a few days ago.'

Suddenly there were any number of waiters close by eager to take our orders; no more of this signalling for twenty minutes before I could attract the attention of one picking his idle way round and over distant recumbent forms. I asked for another beer in the hope that they would then all retreat for a while,

Christel laid a fist on my knee, with her fingers clipping a small envelope. 'Have a look!' she was smiling and there was excitement in her voice. We could have been joyfully examining the rushes of our honeymoon snaps.

I thumbed through the dozen prints with no white edging. The photographs had been taken with a telescopic lens and were views of a man as he left or entered the tall iron gates of a large residence. In three of the shots – from different angles – his facial features were rather clear despite the dark glasses. The Hawaiian shirt was disarming, but this man looked very much indeed like the double-crossing ex-Chinese diplomat, Counsellor Tan. I examined each of the prints again very carefully.

'But it's just not possible,' I said without much conviction in the face of the evidence. 'How can he conceivably be shacked up with a German from Paraguay of all places and who might even be some Waffen SS character seeking a change of air – it's lunatic!'

'But you agree it's Tan?'

'Yes…' I said and put the prints back into the envelope. 'What am I supposed to do about it?'

Christel looked at me sharply. 'I thought you wanted a word with him…'

That made me laugh. It had been nicely put – and

doubly appreciated coming from a foreigner. Without thinking much until it happened, I leaned across and kissed the bemused Christel on the cheek. The contact disturbed me and I had to concentrate hard for a few seconds in order to say something relevant.

'I do "want a word"…' I said, 'but at a time and place of my choosing.' I sipped thoughtfully at my beaker of beer. 'The correct course is to inform the Venezuelan authorities that they are harbouring an international crook who is wanted on suspicion of murder and for swindling the British government out of half a million pounds. But as an unfrocked and very unpopular official, I would be extradited before anybody here took me seriously…'

'Well, we don't want that, do we…?' said Christel slowly as she toyed curiously with one of my plimsolls on the springy poolside turf. 'It appears that this German – a certain Wilhelm Stoeller – has influence here. He moved into a villa in an exclusive area within a day or two of arrival. It will take a week, but we should then have a report from Paraguay which will tell us more. In the meantime…'

Christel paused. She was absent-mindedly filling my brown plimsolls with torn-off blades of very green grass. It was harvest time. 'We need positive identification of Tan,' she said.

'Okay,' I replied quickly. 'I'll stand at the end of the road with a zoom lens until—'

'And we want to know from Tan what really happened to Dobell…'

I hugged my knees and rocked to and fro in agitation.

'For God's sake!' I hissed. 'I can't just walk into some Gestapo hideaway to talk to an unlikely and subtle Chinese lodger who has probably already done for a pal

of mine and who knows that he owes me a lot of money –
even if I could get in. I'd never get out—'

'Do you want to see Tan or not?' It was, neatly
formulated, the key question. And Christel's following
delicate reminder: 'We got you out of France, yes?'
seemed to mean either that the pound of flesh was now
being demanded or that I could count on some more
Russian magic to extract me from any difficulties arising
from a personal encounter with the renegade Maoist.
With the sun, the beer and the temperament of the parties
concerned, I found it impossible to decide which
interpretation was correct.

'Yes…' I said grudgingly, in answer to practically
everything.

We gathered our bits and pieces together and stood
up. I wanted to discuss the nuances of the next move in
the more clinical and less cluttered atmosphere of my
room – where it all should have occurred in the first
place.

Once again, a great many eyes were trained on this
improbable combination as we prepared to leave. Christel
moved so nicely too.

'Hold my hand…' I growled. She looked at me,
surprised for an instant, then she said, 'Yes, please!' at
the same time brushing her face against my shoulder,
which I hadn't bargained for.

For a giddy second I almost forgot what it was I had
to say in passing. The two American beauties lying there
attentively; one in slit-eyed envy at the cut of the lemon-
yellow bikini and the other boggling in amazement at the
hitherto unrecognised attractions of blue football shorts
and the Lawson leer. The professional layabout, in his
animal briefs, I noted with joy, was inadvertently

squeezing suntan cream all over a piece of expensive towelling while he stared open-mouthed at the great departure of the afternoon. Or even of the year. I winked lasciviously at the trio, waving my plimsolls.

'Bye-bye, darlings…'

Chapter 25

ONCE IN THE LIFT that served the accommodation floors from the basement swimming-pool, I disengaged from our charming hand-holding and stood as far as away as possible from this five foot eight inches of golden provocation. But my flow of excited chatter was not very successful in channelling my thoughts entirely to Counsellor Tan.

In the cool, shady hotel room, there was a moment's indecision as I waited for Christel to go into the bathroom to change. But she seemed to be in no hurry to cover up; in fact, while I hastened to fuss in a drawer for a clean shirt, a tiny scrap of lemon-yellow material fluttered down on top of my more mundane and neatly stacked linen. At the same time there was a soft warmth on my back.

I slammed the drawer shut and wheeled round. I was half panic-stricken and half in a rage that fate should put so much provocation in my way. An attitude nicely mixed, no doubt, with the effects of a more chemical reaction. Where was all that debonair control that I had been cultivating of late?

'For God's sake!' I snapped. 'This isn't the moment—'

It was as if the air-conditioning suddenly pumped an ultra chilled draught into the room. A slight hesitation, then Christel pushed herself away.

'It never has been, has it…' she said quietly.

Then she turned and moved unhurriedly, elegantly away from me. And that is something I won't forget for a long time, either. 'Let's get this job finished!' I called after her in what was meant to be a reasonable tone.

In case any reader thinks that I am not making the most of my opportunities, all I can say is that there is probably more to this than meets the eye. Apart from the fact that it was only four hours flying time to Mexico, after all.

Ten minutes later in an atmosphere admittedly a little strained, we discussed in a coldly detached way the details of the next move, and as far as I was concerned, it would be the last for a while. But I didn't tell that to Christel, who contributed to the conversation efficiently by promising local communications and support as necessary. It was unnerving.

We agreed to meet again at the hotel at 6 pm after I had made a preliminary reconnaissance of the current lodgings of ex-Comrade Tan. The address was to the north of the centre in a residential district of tropical gardens called *La Castellana*.

When Christel had left, I went downstairs to a multi-purpose hotel shop and bought a small grip, which would be accepted as hand luggage by any airline. I packed a few belongings that I didn't want to leave behind, but not more obvious things like my toothbrush or the latest in chargeable electric razors. I didn't want to let anybody in the hotel – and least of all Christel, who had a key to my room – know that I had flight in mind.

After a number of little errands in downtown Caracas, by 4 pm I had booked myself onto a VIASA flight calling at Mexico on its way to the US and due to leave at 11.30 that night. I was also the proud driver of a VW 1500 from Avis rent-a-car at the Bello Campo end of one of the main thoroughfares, *Avenida Libertador*, named affectionately after Simon Bolivar, who in the early eighteenth century did as much as anybody to prise Venezuela from Spanish colonial rule. I thought the Liberator's avenue was a fine place to hire my getaway car: it augured well.

I parked the VW conveniently in the city centre, leaving the small grip under the front. seat, and then took a taxi past the lush Country Club district going north towards the massive backdrop of the Avila mountains soaring up into the clouds.

Caraqueños rarely uses street numbers and since anyway I didn't want to give an exact address to my bewildered but friendly taxi driver, we quartered the area of *La Castellana* for half an hour before I located the house. On some pretext I had the driver cruise past the clearly recognisable gates several times.

It was a fine residence set back in beautifully kept grounds. A forty-yard driveway carved through bowling-green turf to the house itself. It was a nicely designed, compact structure of indefinable age, which certainly looked as if it had grown up with the well-matured grounds. Surrounded by thick, high hedging, the property was separated from the next intensely private plot by a ten-foot wall. Some other residences in the area belonged to various embassies and this particular one seemed to be just the place many an ambassador with a guilty conscience would choose as his personal retreat.

As the taxi passed for the last time, I noticed a gardener strolling along the edge of a lawn with a dog at his heels; he was a young, athletic-looking gardener and the dog was a German Shepherd, of course.

In the city centre, I paid off the driver and then collected the VW, which I took back to *La Castellana*, parking it correctly some three hundred yards down the road from Herr Stoeller's mansion. I then had a long walk, fortunately downhill, before I found another taxi to take me to the Tamanaco Hotel. I was half an hour late – again. Christel was already waiting in the room.

'It looks like some grace and favour embassy or official residence – it's well protected and apart from some obvious staff, it's an area patrolled all the time by the police, as you must know... There's only one reasonable way of getting in there – and that's by ringing the bell.'

'Well, good... When—'

'Tonight,' I said quickly. Christel jumped up at that. She had changed into a pair of off-white tight jeans and a casual light-blue shirt with a masculine cut. But the overall effect was unambiguous. In addition, it was all no doubt highly fashionable.

'I told you already this evening – I want to get this business over with...' I added.

'But there's so little time to arrange any help—'

'If it's anything like the last lot, I can do without it,' I said, with vivid memories of a muddy lane on an inland in the middle of the Seine near Paris in faraway France. Christel sat down again and looked at me squarely.

'I prefer, Ken, that you go tomorrow—'

'Now – *tonight!*' I shouted, but it was in good humour.

I moved across to the set-faced Christel and with a winning smile, I brushed my lips across her cheek. 'And I want to borrow your gun for the occasion...'

How ludicrous. But none the less true, for all that.

Here was Lawson, still Her Majesty's loyal servant at heart, kissing his highly sexed temporary KGB case-officer lightly on the cheek and asking for the loan of a gun to stiffen the confidence during an imminent confrontation with a two-faced, double-dealing retired Chinese communist with a lot of recent crime on his conscience – to say nothing of the flaws in his ideological discipline. And a diplomat to boot! What were we coming to!

The loan of a gun, I hoped, for the second time in this affair. The first time round it had not done me a lot of good back there on the *Ile de la Déviation* – by rights somebody should have blown my brains out with it. And what almost certainly unintentionally preserved the author to tell the tale were the low machinations of the monster of St James's Park, Charles Houghton, JP. Yes, he was even a Justice of the Peace in his spare time in the borough of comfortable Churley, Sussex, England.

Christel grabbed my hair. Not roughly, but with just enough tension to remind me who was paying the hotel bill. But in any case I was prepared to do battle – again – to get that gun tonight and, if necessary, render my desirable case-officer senseless so that I could go about my business.

But she released me and went to fish in her copious holiday straw bag, which I had seen at the pool during the afternoon. She handed me a wad of red towelling. I thought for a second that I was dribbling or still had some hamburger relish on my chin. Not so - folded into the towelling was a light .22 pistol and, separately, an absurdly large muffler, which looked like the exhaust pipe of a toy car. The magazine clip was full. It was a perfectly lethal arrangement, properly used, but with me behind the trigger, I would probably do as well to swing with it as to fire it. However, it provided the necessary confidence.

'Thanks – I think—'

'It's only for self-defence, you understand.. He's no good to anybody dead.'

I nodded. It seemed an unnecessarily lurid piece of advice, but later I came to wonder whether I should not have read more into it.

'See you here about 9.30,' I said. This glamorous KGB colonel, or whatever she was, looked at me very straight indeed as I slid out of the room. And yet, as I glanced again at that farewell picture of her as the door closed, composed, very thoughtful, with her neat hands together tapping gently against her chin, I felt a sudden twinge of regret and, laughably, conscience.

Absurd, I said to myself, and at considerable risk, I dallied a little outside the door. Then I heard Christel asking the hotel operator for a Caracas number. Absurd, I told myself again –with a great deal more conviction. Then I rushed downstairs with my confidence hidden under the jacket which I was carrying.

*

For the fifty bolivars I was offering, the taxi-driver would have waited all night in *La Castellana* while I called on my friends. But I merely asked him to wait on an hour and promised a further bonus. On the way up the hill, I had noticed that the VW was still there, we parked under a flowering Araguaney tree and giving Avis the best deal they have ever had. A parked hire-car?

Fifty yards up from the entrance to Comrade Tan's refuge, the taxi pulled in under a street lamp. The driver stuck his face out of the window, settled with the evening paper and told me to take my time.

As I strolled down the well-made road to the front gates of the Stoeller residence, I was beginning to think that Christel had made sense and that tomorrow night would be much better – with the comrades staked out around the place to land a hand. But what could they really do – if there was a scene? Report to Colonel Scholze that Lawson had come unstuck?

No, I told myself, anybody alone in the dark, in a strange city would feel the same. I pushed a bell button set in an illuminated frame to one side of the gates.

I had heard no ringing but a man appeared at the side *portail*. He stared at me through the metal bars of the top half of the solid door. 'Señor?'

'Herr Stoeller is expecting me,' I said. The thirty-year-old man frowned, watching me carefully. 'What is your name please?' he said in English. That frightened me more than a little. 'Klausen,' I said.

He snapped his eyes down and hissed something I didn't understand and I couldn't see what he was looking at. He glanced up again. 'Wait please... I will ask.' He half turned.

'Just a moment,' I said. 'Please show Herr Stoeller this...' In my left hand I thrust my air-ticket towards the bars. As he craned to look, I put the pistol with its toy exhaust against his neck.

'Open the door!' I said softly, with a slight jab into the yielding flesh. He froze, just a little more frightened than I was. 'And control the dog...' I added, still trying to speak without urgency. Dogs sense excitement very quickly. Small, metallic sounds and then the side-gate opened. I watched the man's dark face all the time as I eased my way through.

The Alsatian, a pace away, was bristling, ears laid

back and there was a low, intermittent rasping whine deep in the throat. The Venezuelan had hold of his collar.

'We are going into the house,' I said, 'with the dog – you understand?'

He nodded and began talking to the brute gently. We moved forward. 'Not the front door – a side entrance...'

I kept him two yards ahead of me all the time, with the dog padding around on a short lead, still undecided but no longer in the threshold strike mood that had worried me by the gate.

In the event, we went all the way round to the back of the house because there was no 'side entrance' as such. A crazy-paving patio ran the length of the building and it then it sloped down to a swimming pool with underwater lights. Beyond the pool, the lawn ran back for forty yards to the high wall I had noticed during my first survey from the outside.

The perimeter of the garden was lit artistically by lamps set occasionally along the wall and hanging in the Zapotero and graceful Cedar trees. The still night air was warm and moist – pleasant for any but those who suffocate anywhere south of Brighton – and one might have expected the tall French windows at the back of the residence to be thrown open to greet the softly scented Venezuelan night. However, the windows to what was evidently the principal living area were heavily curtained. Light showed at the edges of the thick material.

I could hear the soft purr of an air-conditioning unit somewhere but I couldn't see it. Once a shadow flickered in the crack of light below the curtains, but there were no handy gaps in the drapes – which most investigators seem to find on these occasions – giving a preliminary view of the excitement inside.

We came to the tradesmen's entrance, which led to the kitchen area, if some fascinating cooking smells were any guide. Adolfo seemed to be dragging his steps, so I prodded him lightly with the Russian technology conveniently covered by the jacket folded over my arm. 'In we go,' I said in an encouraging tone.

Past some service offices which included a 'cellar' with only a dozen or so bottles in the racks we trooped into a modern kitchen layout. The Alsatian was at our heels and now in a better temper; suspicion of me being overlaid, no doubt, by the more fundamental prospects of kitchen scraps.

An old man with weepy eyes was tending to various copper pots on a large cooking range. Judging from the smells of baking sea food and *creole* sauce, somebody was soon going to enjoy a marvellous *cazuela de mariscos*.

The old man looked at home in the kitchen. His general bearing, the way he checked the dishes, the jet-black apron tied around his waist gave him the air of a priceless expert. His large fluffy white moustache was stained at the bottom edge from testing the sauces.

How much he could see I don't know, but he didn't react to our arrival at all. Adolfo's large brown eyes must have been orbiting to convey all sorts of messages, but the old man was quite rightly much more interested in his simmering pots of this and that.

The dog was quite diverted by now, trotting from one end of the kitchen to the other and swinging his tail expectantly. Any moment he could stop and bark, demanding his dues. 'Give the dog something to keep him quiet,' I said to Adolfo.

I watched him carefully as he found some meat

scraps and then there was a delay as he searched for an appropriate dish.

'Anything will do!' I said sharply. But it was too late. The Alsatian's stomach got the better of his training and he started to bark in excitement.

'Give it to him on the floor!' I snapped. The Venezuelan was staring at me with panic in his face, fearing that the noise was his death knoll.

'The dog gulped at the bonus in a corner. The cook spared us a casual glance, wiping his tired eyes with his apron, as Adolfo and I walked through the kitchen into a ten-yard passageway. Just as I closed the door behind me, the other end of the corridor opened.

Still wearing dark glassed and a sports shirt, Counsellor Tan stepped from a room with a glass in his hand and his tentative manner was of somebody bent on enquiry.

Adolfo just in front of us stopped dead. Tan peered a little to one side to get a better view of me. At what moment recognition came was difficult to tell; certainly his face didn't change. But his hand was suddenly shining with spilt champagne from the tall, fluted glass he was carrying.

I could have killed him then and there with a lot less noise than the barking of the Alsatian a moment ago that had attracted his attention. But there were a number of questions still to be answered.

Nobody moved for some seconds. Except Adolfo – and the trembling of his legs was involuntary. Tan's immobile stupefaction seemed to be infectious because although I had planned several alternative pungent opening lines, none of these, in the event, came suavely to my lips. I didn't even think about it consciously.

'I want a word with you,' I said. And even that was

fair Christel's understated formula!

With his free hand Tan removed his dark glasses in a '*Me voilà*' gesture.

'Well, Mr Lawson, you were expected – but not quite so soon as this...' It was the cool, careful voice from the *Ile de la Déviation*, when Tan had very much been the master of the situation. But, goddamit, I thought things had developed a little since then!

A half-formed retort died on my lips. From the open door behind Tan, a very cultured voice exclaimed:

'Good heavens! What a... what a remarkable effort!'

I don't really know whether it was because some small, un-dusted corner of my mind had already been theorising on the subject, or whether it was just because I was fed up with shocks in this case, but that voice seemed to cause me no particular surprise.

He came out and stood just a little behind the Chinese, dressed in well-cut beige slacks and a colourful silk shirt; he, too, had a glass in one hand and in the other a black cigarette in an ivory holder.

'Lopez – clear off! Don't stand there gawping! And tell Pedro there's a guest for dinner!'

Lopez, for such he was apparently called, and not Adolfo, ducked round me like a startled rabbit – except that he was muttering, 'Si, señor!' several times, And I was left standing all keyed-up in that passageway with my jacket still hiding a lethal Soviet contribution to my self-defence.

'For goodness sake – come in, man, come in and have a drink!'

If there was something that Henry Dobell had always been able to do disarmingly well, it was to cope with the unexpected.

Chapter 26

STRICTLY SPEAKING, any ideas of wreaking a terrible vengeance on Tan were in one sense irrelevant – because he had not after all done away with colleague Dobell, who was standing there to prove it, generously pouring *Moët & Chandon* into a third glass for the unexpected visitor.

The gun was therefore something of an embarrassment. I had already refused to shake hands with anybody – 'until I've had a drink or two' – and moreover I had more or less pushed the solicitous Chinese away when he made a move to take my coat.

Dobell placed the glass on a table by the side of a soft leather-clad armchair. 'Sit down, Ken - relax ...!' he said, and then went back to join Tan already squatting on a plush sofa in the same style. A new hi-fi ensemble, not yet properly installed by the new tenants, was spread on the floor but connected up and functioning quietly. The background music for this journey's end was Bach's Toccata and Fugue in D Minor – improvisation and flight, roughly speaking. I looked at my watch. An hour and a half before *my* flight took off for Mexico.

'Welcome to Venezuela, Ken,' said Henry Dobell, raising his glass. I drank to that and then placed my jacket on the arm of the chair leaving the gun obscenely exposed in my lap. There was still a lot of straight talking to be done.

Tan looked anxious and fidgeted nervously with the piece of fluted crystal in his hand. Dobell moved eagerly around, topping up the glasses. Seated again, he said: 'You want to know why, of course...'

'That for a start,' I said. 'And let's not fool around – I want the real story...' I think I glanced involuntarily at the weapon across my knees. Dobell stared at the item, affecting keen interest.

'Where the devil did you get that?' he asked. 'It's not one of ours!' The tone was one of scandalised reproach.

'It's Russian,' I said. 'And it works...' The champagne was probably going to my head. I lined the thing up casually across the room and fired. No more than a sharp cough from a big man but simultaneously a tall vase containing orange blossoms and Calla Lilies standing on the floor twelve feet away exploded with a bang, leaving a kaleidoscope of flowers, splintered pottery and a creeping puddle of water.

Tan leapt to his feet, spilling more of his champagne, but Dobell just looked at me with apparently genuine respect.

'You must have been practising – that's quite good shooting...'

'I want the real story!' I repeated. I didn't tell him that I had been aiming at the clock on the mantelpiece. Behind me the door suddenly opened and wide-eyed Adolfo-Lopez was there with the straining Alsatian on a short lead.

'Tell Pedro we'll be eating in about half an hour,' said Dobell as if he had just rung the service bell. The Venezuelan hesitated and there was some snuffling noise by my chair.

Dobell stood up. 'Well, go on!' he said sharply. 'And what is that dog doing in here? Put him outside where he belongs!'

Dobell moved across to the record-player on the floor and turned the disk over. 'You don't mind this music, do you...' he said. It wasn't exactly a question. I felt that after my display of fine marksmanship I probably could have had my favourite Beatles LP if necessary.

'It's quite simple,' said Dobell settling down again. He shot a quick accomplice's smile at Tan, that slender, handsome Chinese. 'Tan here—' he smiled again at the Chinese, 'wanted to come over... I was quite sure and made the appropriate recommendations. But Houghton told me it was politically unacceptable and instead proposed a course which I felt was immoral—'

'That Tan should work for us with the promise of a nonexistent eventual haven in the UK...' I had done my homework, of course.

'Yes, that's about it...' Dobell looked at me steadily. 'I thought it was wrong in principle –and I just couldn't do it. The other event was critical for me...' He stopped, but I had the impression that it was a studied hesitation to persuade me of an embarrassment he didn't feel – or no longer felt.

'As you must know by now, the Russians compromised me in Bangkok—'

'For God's sake, Henry, every other officer has a skeleton in the cupboard and many fornicate with London's consent – why should *you* be so sensitive!'

Dobell looked at me with an odd, tolerant expression as if I belonged to a race apart. I suddenly felt brutish and uncomprehending.

'It wasn't so simple... not so simple.' Henry Dobell was saying, and was no longer looking at me. He had turned towards his accomplice with a rueful smile. I stared first at Dobell and then at Tan, whose eyes were lowered. Then suddenly I understood. I gulped inelegantly at the champagne.

'All right,' I said with as much casualness as I could muster.

'Tan had nothing to do with that, you know,' said Dobell quickly. 'I had a Thai friend... He must have been very careless or perhaps the Russians got to him by sheer chance. But when I discovered that they had been... monitoring me in Bangkok, I decided that it was time to move.'

'And so you made a proposition to Comrade Tan that you *both* defect – or rather, retire to a third country.'

Dobell's assessment of Tan had been remarkably perceptive; of course, he was well-placed to recognise homosexual tendencies – if the picture in front of me was what it seemed.

My feeling of crisp authority suddenly began to wane with onset of embarrassment. I am just not at ease knowing that I'm in this sort of company; 'knowing' is the key word – without such knowledge normality would reign. I could even play chess, for example.

.'Supposing, to take a flexible view,' I said, pulling myself together bravely, 'we say that your disappearance caused chiefly bureaucratic inconveniences and that it is perhaps your own affair, the scene changes, doesn't it, when you cheat HMG out of £400,000.'

'It was a well-considered figure,' said Dobell blandly. 'If I had gone to London with the whole story, I would have been out on my neck overnight with no pension— even in these enlightened days. This seemed unjust – I had given twenty-five years service, most of it at least satisfactory and—'

'You decided to take your pension in a lump sum,' I said, doing some quick sums in my head. Ludicrous though it was, I was now quibbling over the size of the loot!

'Assuming you live another twenty years, your retirement salary would be about £7,000 – that accounts for £140,000... Now, supposing friend Tan here is entitled to his five bob for aiding and abetting this rotten fraud, that still leaves a great deal of money unaccounted for...'

'I am Wilhelm Stoeller, a German national but with no Gestapo connections, late of Paraguay – all that took forceful negotiation and required... er... required support, or financing if you wish...'

'Bribes!' I said sharply. Dobell got up and went round with the bottle again. Tan put a hand over his glass in refusal. I couldn't get enough – and the Moët was running out. I hoped there was an extra bottle on ice in the kitchen.

'Ken, there was a time when you were a rather broad-minded and imaginative operative of that villainous and occasionally effective outfit WRU... You even tickled HMG into giving you – yes, you too – a doubtful *ex gratia* payment in lieu of pension – why have you become so stuffy—'

'*For crissake!*' I roared. 'I have been near killed on this exercise, not to mention being savagely beaten up twice and I can expect insensitive, homicidal MI6 hirelings and others creeping down from the Sierra Madre towards my peaceful hacienda for months to come! Yes, I've grown stuffy...'

Both Dobell and Tan looked at me in surprise. Dobell even seemed concerned. What Tan was really thinking I couldn't tell because he had put his dark glasses on again. 'I don't understand,' he said.

'Never mind... A few more details – how was the

substitution of the bag in the boat done?'

'I was piloting the launch,' said Dobell. 'As soon as Tan saw you drop the bag he signalled and I took off with the skiff in tow... I had a wet-suit – I had learned a little about diving while in Thailand. Once in midstream I fixed the rudder for the long, straight part of the river, swapped the bags and swam to the shore. Not a great exploit really...'

'The *patron* of Le Refuge is a friend of yours? – you were in France a year ago,' I said.

Dobell looked at me very straight for a moment and then he smiled. Tan was coughing quietly to himself.

'You don't disappoint me after all, Ken – you have a certain flair—'

'*Flair*?' I shouted. 'That thug of an ex-*Légionnaire* virtually spat in my eye—'

'I should apologise for that,' interrupted Dobell in that tone of quiet control, which I knew for sure had subdued much wilder men than me. 'I fabricated a story involving you in some ugly Vietnam thing and tied Tan into it as a Vietnamese friend... I had done the *patron* a few favours a long time ago when he had another place in Paris – he was glad to help...'

'I need more than an apology,' I said sourly. 'But first tell me why you of all people could have been so careless in Bangkok to let the Russians trail you all over town—'

'Careless?' Dobell smiled. 'It was deliberate, my friend, deliberate...'

I leaned forward a little in the chair, fascinated. The gun was dangling between my knees. 'Go on...'

'Well, the Thai boy was a real mistake, of course, but once I discovered that they had got that, I made sure they got a great deal more. I knew that they would make a major effort to watch me all the time. So I led them to Tan – which must have made the lights burn all night in the Soviet Embassy, And, finally, of course, we were careful to let them watch the abduction. Needless to say Tan was alone in the van, but we staged it with a lot of noise to suggest more people. I thought that, in the circumstances, the Russians would make the best possible witnesses... I take it they went straight to our Ambassador with the story?'

'Yes,' I said shortly. In fact, the information had been delivered in London, but Dobell was essentially right. He had been very clever indeed, I tried not to dwell on the fact that he had swindled the government out of a fortune; nor that his retirement villa (though less charming) oddly called to mind a certain hacienda in Mexico. In passing, I was feeling vexed with that man Bach still going strong on the floor with another of his wretched fugues – "Fugue: a subject introduced by one of the parts and successively taken up by the others". Yes, Dobell's operations had a certain style, although I didn't accept his facile pension calculations (neither did he, I was sure). There was only one thing seriously wrong with Dobell's plotting as far as I was concerned. Thinking about it gave an edge to my voice in which, until then, the tone of menace and outrage had been flagging.

'You *used* me...' I said accusingly in the way that everybody else says it when the occasion demands. But it's a poor formula – an admission of gullibility. I now wished I hadn't said it.

'Yes, I'm sorry...' Dobell remarked casually. 'Er... how much are they paying you for this tripping around?' Regrettably, his innocent use of the present tense was unjustified.

'Houghton offered me five thousand pounds for a three-month contract and—'

'That's rather generous.'

'But I only squeezed £2500 advance out of Houghton and in the circumstances, I'm unlikely to get the rest ... Because, whether he really believes it or not, Houghton – who as you know has long since been waiting to clobber me – will certainly implicate me in the loss of the so-called ransom money... There's only the word of Ian Potter in Paris and even he will probably have his doubts – especially when the Russians start telling more of the story. It will be clear to all that I didn't report everything which came to my notice...'

'What do you mean?' Dobell fixed another black Sobranie in his ivory cigarette holder, which gave him an appropriate air of wise concentration.

'Do you know, Henry,' I said very deliberately. 'Back in sultry Bangkok, I concluded that you were ill-advisedly using these hotel rooms for... non-official purposes, but I kept quiet because I didn't want to ruin your reputation and career – it's laughable, isn't it!'

There was a brief silence and nobody laughed. ''You just *used* me,' I added. There it was again!

Dobell looked uncomfortable for a fleeting moment but his Chinese friend just stared at me impassively.

'Don't be so glum, Ken, it's not like you!' Dobell said breezily and stood up. He stepped deliberately over the hi-fi equipment on the floor and moved towards a heavy antique writing desk against the wall. On the way, he scuffed at some bits of wet pottery strewn on the well-polished parquet floor, tut-tutting as he went.

Every nerve in my body told me to stand up as well.

But I stayed where I was, alert, nervous and not wanting to betray it to this pair of unreasonably relaxed music-lovers. Dobell had his back to me at the desk and I couldn't see what he was doing.

'Remember, Henry, champagne or not, I'm a real menace with this gun!'

Dobell chuckled and went on with what he was doing, but at least Tan sat up a little straighter among the soft, sighing leather cushions of the sofa. Dobell came back and put two neatly bound packs of US currency on the table by my chair.

'There's ten thousand dollars – a bit more than what is due to you from Houghton…'

I looked at Dobell blankly.

'Take it,' he said. 'After all, it's Houghton's SOF money, no doubt… Put it away and then let's have dinner!'

My face evidently wasn't betraying the right signs of gratitude. Dobell continued with his gentle patter: 'Stay here a while – there's lots of room… Have a holiday… And I understand the town is full of… of beautiful distractions!'

I stood up quickly and again folded my coat over the miraculous lifesaver, the butt of which was now very hot and wet in my hand. I left the nice, crisp-looking bundles where they were.

'I'm leaving for Mexico tonight…'

An instant's hesitation then Dobell, without being asked, moved towards the door with Tan close behind him.

'I thought you might say something like that…' he remarked.

In the pillared porch-way there was another stand-still

silence while the three of us looked at one another, each putting his own interpretation on the sort of stalemate we had reached.

'You realise that you will have a number of other visitors before too long…' I said.

'But what can anybody do?' said Dobell. 'We're well protected – Tan, living here incognito, has been granted political asylum and quite apart from the… influence I've brought to bear, I'm too useful as an adviser to the Ministry of the Interior for there to be any question of extradition or anything of that sort...'

Dobell was smiling good-humouredly at me and he went on smiling when I said, 'Still, I'd lock your bedroom door at nights…'

I had even turned to leave when the noise of a car door slamming just outside the gates stopped me in my tracks.

The side *portail* opened immediately. A thickset man in his early fifties, dressed in a lightweight dark suit, walked towards the porch-way with a hand raised in greeting. It wasn't quite a Nazi salute and his moustache was of the drooping, fashionable variety.

He was smiling aimlessly at the new tenants of *La Castellana* residence. But his eyes were hard and searching when he turned to me.

*

'Colonel Martinez, this is an old friend of mine… Karl, from Munchen… He's just leaving unfortunately.'

In some confusion, I wondered whether to transfer the coat and gun to the other arm so that I could shake the preferred hand. I decided not – it wasn't a hand I particularly wanted to shake. I turned to leave.

'My departure is no reflection on your arrival, Colonel.' I gave a sickly smile over my shoulder. What else do you say to the Deputy Chief of the Secret Police? Especially as I had noticed out of the corner of my eye Dobell giving a slight 'okay' nod in answer to what must have been an enquiring look from the Colonel – who was doubtless there to check on reports of a stranger in *La Castellana*.

As I went through the gate only Dobell called out, '*Buenos noches!*' He was consistently polite, Dobell.

I walked up the road, pausing on the lush verge for a mundane need. As I trudged away, I reflected that Dobell could not have made a better choice of intermediary than the flexible, long-suffering and complaisant Lawson.

Somewhat to my surprise, the taxi was still there. The driver was laid out along the front seats, snoring noisily. I shook him awake and got in beside him, flashing another 50 B. bonus. 'Down the hill a bit – stop when I tell you... You then drive on back to the hotel – okay?'

Of course it was 'okay'; he had never had such a generous client. So off we went. As I quickly slid out of the taxi, I said to the driver, 'Pick me up tomorrow morning at the hotel and there will be another 50 Bs...'

'*Si, si señor!*' He was mine for a week.

There was only a second to spare. As I hung back in the shadows of the roadside vegetation, first a motorcyclist went by and then a car in which there were at least three people.

I walked back up the road to the VW. I got into the car and folded my coat over the weapon on the front passenger seat. I was wondering whether to try and keep the gun as a souvenir or throw it away. I would decide during the drive.

I headed up the hill in the opposite direction to the convoy which had just gone down. In a few minutes I arrived at the Cota Mil, a highway running along the lower reaches of the Avila mountain range and which, in a wide detour, would take me to Maiquetía Airport. There was an hour before my flight's scheduled take-off, so I drove slowly on the near deserted road.

Both front windows were open of course, and I had an elbow on the door ledge, relaxed now and half convincing myself that the affair had satisfactorily wound up with less grief and slaughter than there might have been – given the nature of the participants. Down to the left, the lights of the city glittered over a panorama which stretched for miles.

Then I became aware that something was bothering me. For a second or two I couldn't identify it. Suddenly I knew what it was and instinctively I started to brake the car. Almost at the same moment when I recognised the faint trace of Lanvin's expensive little bottle, I felt form, cool fingers gripping the back of my shirt collar, pulling my tie into my throat. A hand snaked down to retrieve the gun under the jacket.

'This is not the way to the hotel,' said Christel Scholze and I felt something hard pushed against my neck. 'Pull in there – just ahead!'

Chapter 27

'**G**ET OUT…'

I had driven compliantly into one of the parking bays on the downhill aside of the Cota Mil from where *Caraqueños* and visitors admire the view of the city spread below.

I got out as instructed and moved to the parapet. The terrain shelved down very steeply; you wouldn't plunge to your death from there but an inert body would conveniently roll 200 feet or more into the scrub at the bottom,

Christel, in her well-cut jeans, walked round to the edge too; she stood a pace or two away, leaning against the parapet, watching me carefully. It was the pose that counts among your holiday snaps – if you are lucky enough to have a tall, slim blonde with a great deal of poise in your baggage. Christel even had her left hand resting across her shopping bag placed on the parapet. The only unusual feature – apart from the fact that this striking figure would command more attention than most – was the Made-in-the-USSR automatic with a muffle on the snout which was being held down against her right thigh. This was presumably to prevent the barrel glinting in the Venezuelan moonlight. Not that there was anybody around to alarm. Except me.

'Where were you going?'

'To the airport.'

There was a pause while that sunk in, although Christel had probably guessed my plans.

'What about your report on what you found in the house?'

'I was going to send you a postcard—'

'*Verdammt!* It's not funny – tell me what happened!' Her face showed that she was very angry indeed. Her right hand suddenly moved, too, but it may have been an involuntary gesture. It was the sort of thing one notices, however. I shrugged and sighed.

'They are both there... The German "Stoeller" is Dobell, and the Chinese you photographed is Tan. But they are untouchable – protected. Dobell is hand in glove with the police and Tan has political asylum...'

Christel stared at me with shining eyes and slowly a wry smile relaxed her mouth. 'So...' she mused, 'Dobell arranged his own kidnapping... But how did he involve Tan?'

'The Chinese wanted to defect and evidently he didn't much care where he went.' I glanced at my match. 'Right,' I added, pushing myself away from the parapet, 'that's it... I've done my job and I'm off—'

'Stay where you are!' Christel's tone was sharp and it had authority – even without that ugly-looking gun .being trained on my midriff. 'There is some unfinished business—'

'The hell there is!' I exclaimed. 'The plane leaves in forty-five minutes and I intend to be on it!'

'You are a cheap double-crossing bastard yourself, aren't you! We – I – got you out of France in return for your cooperation... You don't run out on me like that. Morally, you owe me—'

'Don't lecture me on morals!' I snapped furiously. 'You wanted Dobell to be found not for any humanitarian motives, not even because you were frightened of what he might tell the Chinese – but you wanted him so that you could then blackmail him as a homosexual – with all that dirty evidence so carefully collected in Bangkok! And you personally knew what was going on – "Just gave the tapes to Alex" – balls!'

We glared at one another. I was breathless with rage and shaking a little. The gun in Christel's hand moved as much as an anvil.

'I told you once that I needed help…' she said. Her voice had changed but that was all.

'I don't even know your real name—'

'Anna Lehmann...'

This immediate revelation put us off my stride. Oh God, I didn't want to know about it! I didn't want to hear about it! I didn't want to hear how her sister back in Leipzig was living in the shadow of reprisals from the dreaded East German Security Police if Christel – Anna, now – didn't continue to work for the fraternal KGB! Nor did I want to be told that she was only doing it because they promised that her four-year-old son cooped up in a Dresden Workers' crèche would soon be allowed to join Mama in the glittering West – I didn't want to know about this or any other unlikely tales. Let her try it on some other fellow – let him sort out what was believable and what was not! I'd had enough of this case.

'I'm going to Mexico any moment now,' I said. 'Why don't you call on Ian Potter in Paris – he's a decent… a human sort of chap. He'll give you a fair hearing!'

For a moment she looked uncertain; then her mouth hardened in resolve and there may have been bitterness in her eyes. I didn't know whether the gun was really being pointed at me because of failure to comply with all the KGB requirements she had in mind, whether it was my unwillingness to respond to her alleged need of 'help', or whether, simply, it was that I had managed – against all the odds – to keep my hands off her during our mainly pleasant acquaintance. But I was acutely reminded of what is said of 'a woman scorned'...

'You are a real bastard,' she said with feeling.

'Yes…'

I turned on my heel and walked across to the car.

Whether she pulled the trigger or not, I will never know. As I drove off, I dusted my handkerchief out of the window in farewell and at the same time nine .22 cartridges (the other spent one Dobell would doubtless find in due course and keep as a souvenir) fell out and bounced all over the well-made surface of the Cota Mil highway.

Anna, alias Christel, would have a lonely half an hour's walk in the dark, but I thought she could probably take care of herself.

*

It was ten minutes after boarding time for the Mexico flight when I arrived at Maiquetía Airport; but with only hand-luggage to check, I was allowed to scramble onto that plane.

During a refuelling stop in Panama, I visited the Post Office in the small bazaar-like terminal building. After scrapping two drafts, I handed to the incredulous but good-humoured clerk a telegram addressed to: 'Charles Houghton, Esq., JP, Foreign Office, London'. (Houghton, of course, didn't live at the Foreign Office and it would upset everybody, but they knew where to find him). The text read:

'Suspects have fled to Mexico. Am still following of course. (Signed) Your Ken.'

I didn't believe that this would ensure that my back pay would arrive in the next post, but I thought that Houghton would want to know that I was alive and well.

about the author

DENIS MILLER was born and educated in the UK where he studied Oriental Languages at Cambridge University. He became a freelance journalist working for a press ranging from *The Far Eastern Economic Review*, *Le Monde Diplomatique* to the UK's *The Countryman*.

In a parallel career, he was Government-employed in the China field for some twenty years. With work in the Far East and in Europe, the variety of his particular experience is probably unique. After a period at GCHQ as a Chinese linguist, he spent time with three different Western Services: MI6, the Australian Secret Intelligence Service (ASIS) and the CIA. He is now retired in France, and writing another novel.

Denis Miller's other fiction includes *The Chinese Jade Affair* and *Alle Spie Piace Formosa* (Mondadori, Milan), *Diplomatic Traffic* (New English Library), and *A Spell in Normandy* (Kédéa Editions, Paris).

china **scoop** by denis **miller**

'An elegant and nicely crafted thriller.' *Nick Webb*

'An action-packed political thriller with great background locations and charismatic characters. Well written by an ex-agent who has worked for several secret service agencies. A highly enjoyable read with an enthralling story coming out of China.' *Orpheus*

'I enjoyed this book. Fast-moving and speculative. An enjoyable and captivating read.' – *E. Wood*

'Transports one back to the Far East, those inscrutable Chinese, the tensions in the 1970s – those of us who ever visited the Communist Store in Hong Kong with Mao's little red book and ivory carvings of Mao talking to the people will enjoy this thriller and the hidden agendas of Governments.' – *Orient*